KAPI]

MW00974141

KYIRUX: THE MESSAGE OF PASCAL

ISBN- 978-0-557-40468-1

BY KAPIEL RAAJ

Kirtiker@gmail.com

www.KRSNOVELS.com

An ancient device, with unknown origins will change the life of entire planet.

What will be found inside it may be beyond comprehension.

A MESSAGE THAT WILL CHANGE US ALL

KAPIEL RAAJ

KAPIEL RAAJ

A NOVEL

CHAPTER 1
STEPS OF GOD

Deep breathing could be heard as it approached the doors of the ship. Automatically opening in a most peculiar fashion, and dissolving into thin air, the doors opened. No sooner than this occurred, the creature witnessed a magnificent sunset the naked eye had never seen.

The sun was on the horizon behind untainted, white, icy mountains. On the snow-covered ground, the white padded legs of the creature landed on surface; a thick, protective, glossy, and shiny material encompassed them.

Scanning the body of the white rubbery alien which had stepped out of the ship was a layer of four tubes in the knee region containing a blue liquid. The suit wasn't different from that of a current earthy astronaut. It had the same thick material, but the entire body was made of animated logos and symbols. One symbol stood out more than the rest "SYIRUX-82," which animated itself redundantly.

The peculiar creature held a folded piece of paper in his hand that displayed objects and symbols animating inside. The main mystery lay in the creature's head, but it was covered all around with thick golden glass that showed a reflection of icy mountains and the setting sun. The alien commenced to walk forward. He took seven to ten steps onto the ground and stopped. After a few moments, he unfolded the sheet.

The sheet became a computer screen, which displayed all the landscape levels and temperatures with humidity. Panning the sheet at a 180-degree direction, graphs and the numbering began to change. But, the most fascinating aspect was, the measurements were exactly like the ones used on Earth in current times. The language that appeared on the chart was English. The creature reached for a green button on the side of his left leg and pressed it.

After a few moments, the main door opened and three other entities came out wearing the same exact suit, however in different colors scheme and logos.

The mysterious astronaut creature that first took the step on Earth surface, folded the computer, and placed it in his pocket. He reached for his helmet with both hands and simultaneously pressed a golden button on each side of his helmet. Steam of gas shot out from both ends and slowly the golden glass began to disappear, dissolving into thin air.

The figure turned out to look human, but slightly different in features. He stood like a captain and commander-in-chief, as his hair was golden in color and his bright blue eyes sparkled from the dimming sunlight. He glanced over towards the sunset with an ardent look. It seemed as though it was the first time he was viewing such a scene. He knew it had been light years since he last witnessed any sunset. He wanted to cherish the moment by not blinking his eyelids for a single second. It perhaps reminded him of home, its life and its happiness.

He then spoke to himself, *"this must be heaven."*

CHAPTER 1-B

THE RISING AGE

It was dark, with tiny, thin valleys of lava flowing like veins inside a human brain. The planet was cooling down from a collision between our sun and a much larger star. It had a thin, yellow ozone layer; quite different from planet earth, which itself was a tiny ball of brown fur in comparison to this huge, mystical dark body.

The dark planet also carried a small strange moon, which really wasn't a moon at all. It was actually a burning ball of fire that refused to cool down. The planet had an elliptical orbit around our sun, and it seemed to defy the standard physical behavior of a massive heavenly body.

∑ Years ago

All there was was darkness and nothing more. A pure black sheet of infinity proportion had swallowed time and space. A stillness of this magnitude could only be imagined but never experienced.

Time was undetectable in this place. It had no meaning to this entity of darkness, which had no galaxies, planets, stars, dark-matter, black holes, pulsars and quasars. It was just complete darkness and silence. Even God doesn't exist in this matrix.

Goggles and goggles, octillion light years away in darkness where even distance couldn't be calculated, and neither it mattered; something happened. It was unexplainable and undetectable, but it did occur. No one was there to witness it, and no one will ever be able to fathom its reality. But even darkness had weight. It was growing.

Darkness itself was a compound, and once it reached beyond the tolerable amount no larger than Quantum ascertain; Universe happened. In less than one-trillionth of a second light was born. It eclipsed darkness and expanded itself for quindecillion light years, giving birth to billions and trillions of galaxies, and within those galaxies; were stars, gasses and destruction.

One of these stars, which lay in the center of the Universe, occupies 1.5% of matter. Other, much microscopic stars such as our sun, found its home in this strange phenomenon, at the edge of the galaxy. Once settled, it stood still without moving or rotating, but only burning loud and bright. It had no reason to be present, and, no mission to accomplish. It just stood still without any purpose. While it kept burning itself, another gas giant came and collided with our sun. Matter circulating this new and bigger star became bounded by its immense gravity. Masses plowed into each other. Planets were born. One particular planet, seven times larger than Jupiter, took a very unique and strange orbit. Instead of revolving horizontally around the sun, it orbited vertically.

Time- 500,000,000 years ago

The rock was a 100-mile wide meteoroid that had traveled approximately 755 million miles from planet Saturn. As it slowly penetrated through the surface, burning debris and ashes crashed into planet earth's atmosphere with a velocity of great magnitude. The rock dispersed throughout the blue planet.

After ephemeral moments of abruptness and chaos there was a sudden silence, which engulfed earth for five seconds. Thereafter, it began to quiver as a huge cloud of fire and dust moved in from middle of the ocean across the entire globe. At this moment in time all the continent were joined together in a one gigantic land. The giant green land turned to oceans of fire, covering the mother earth, turning it into a ball of fire in a matter of minutes.

There was no disparity in the appearance of sun and earth, since they looked as though they were both one entity, belonging to the same family of heavenly bodies of fire and destruction. Furthermore, anything that was ever alive and breathing on the planet's surface had vanished into oblivion, never to reappear or to be born ever again.

Without any doubt or struggle, earth kept revolving around the sun. The inferno on the planet's surface diminished. The North Pole, which had just been a land of hell and fire, gave way to a glimpse of an icy kingdom as small clusters of ice emerged and gradually dispersed throughout the planet.

Moving away from the place called home into some oblivion, earth began to get small in size. However, before getting too far, a strange object sped its way towards the planet.

It was a huge, rectangular, brown cube with dark origin and small tiny yellow lights that were lit throughout. The lower back-edge of the golden object had a radiant glow from a yellow laser directly below the symbol "SYIRUX-82."

Above the atmosphere of earth hovered this unusual alien craft, looking and observing our planet as it remained completely still. A tiny square piece of the spacecraft detached itself from the ship much like a piece of cake removes itself from the whole.

The small brown-box like object above earth morphed itself into a disk and vanished inside the planet's surface at an unthinkable speed. At this moment, the planet had a thick layer of ice above a landmass, which after millions of years would be called "United States of America".

It resembled a computer screen, exhibiting upon a transparent piece of glass that was projected by a blue laser light from beneath. The screen displayed heat signatures and different levels of mountain ranges, which may be that of planet earth. A finger more beautiful than that of humans, worked on a Kiosk screen. The finger was pale brown with a soothing pink and light green light glowing from within. The nails on the finger were glossy and artificial in look. It had three joints instead of two like of humans. The finger hovered over the glass screen and clicked on the heat signature of mountain ranges, and a small popup window appeared showing readings of oxygen, carbon dioxide, gravity level, and magnetic pull of the planet.

The spaceship orbited around earth's surface, quickly changing its texture from metal into pure diamond, which could penetrate through planet's atmosphere without causing any damage to the ship's exterior. The craft surpassed the beauty of our own planet as sunlight hit its outer shell. It tilted itself towards Earth's surface and within half a second sped into the dense and thick clouds in the atmosphere. Descending downward, the icy land began to show more details each and every second.

Deep breathing of a creature underneath its glass helmet could be heard as it approached the doors of the ship.

CHAPTER 2
THE LAST FACE-OFF

National Space Center
Huston, TX 1999

Jack Crawford sat at a dusty desk scattered with files and papers. He scratched his unwashed hair, as he looked at his reflection on a computer monitor and felt the scruff of his beard. A thought crept into his head. *What the hell am I doing here? I'm sure, I would've been much happier as a construction worker.* He knew what he had gotten himself into, but now, his mind had one way of getting out: walking out the door and never looking back. His somber look could no longer hide within.

The bookshelf behind him spoke loudly of his personality and thoughts. All he had were mythological books on ancient occultisms, numerology, astrology and mystical cultures like Mayans and Hinduism.

Jack glanced over to the picture of him and his wife Tracy, but nothing positive came to his mind. Not even a smiling gesture or calmness. It reminded him of being in a worst situation than this present place. He might have thought of perhaps leaving both of these dilemmas to the void of Universe. His attire seemed like he hadn't gone home or had any sleep within the past seventy two hours.

Jack wasn't motivated or willing to do anything productive. He knew he was wasting away at the agency. Since he began five years ago, no one cared to take him seriously. He was bound by rules and guidelines, which he resented by heart. Rubbing his finger on his lips, he glanced over to the window where a blurred figure was running towards his office.

Kelly rushed inside the office calling Jack's name before she even opened the door. "Jack, what the hell are you doing? They are waiting for you," she said aggressively.

He glanced at her and looked back at his reflection on monitor. "Did you even take a shower today?" Kelly asked.

"What for?" Jack replied, as he was reluctant to see anyone; but he stood up, picked up a tie and his wrinkled jacket, and walked out of office without paying any attention to Kelly.

Walking in hallway Kelly noticed Jack was walking out without his paper or laptop. "You're going to a presentation empty handed?"

"Do I need a date or something to escort me to the meeting?" Jack replied humorously as he wanted to walk by himself, lost in his thoughts and dilemmas as he was born on the 7th day, and, according to numerology, people born on the 7th needed much time to themselves, and they loved being alone. The world laughed at 7's because they were different, but, 7's had the last laugh because everyone else was the same.

"Perhaps a notepad would look professional," said Kelly as she walked ahead arrogantly.

"For these clowns, you've got to be kidding me."

Standing amongst 25 senior level scientists, Jack in a messy shirt and jacket, with a tie loosened around his neck, explained a problem to board-members and executives; a problem that only he knew of.

"It's coming soon," said Jack standing in front of a wide chalkboard filled with myriads of mathematical equations.

"I'm really not sure if it has intelligent life on it, but I know it's going to happen very soon."

Through the glass window viewing was Clark Gabriel and Jay Michael Verma, witnessing Jack being pounded by these so-called corporate intellects. Clark and Jay weren't the most popular or the most important figures at the facility, but more of just spectators at hearings, who were also good friends of Jack and brilliant underappreciated minds. Chortling Clark and Jay still managed to keep up a smile to support their eccentric friend.

Karen, one of the members on Board of Directors suddenly spoke up, "Can you care to explain who is coming?"

"This dark planet," Jack replied bluntly and candidly at which point Karen leaned back on her chair, while some mumblings were heard in the background.

"I am sorry. I just feel that I need to find more information on the data you are discussing and how exactly you came about reaching this conclusion," said Ronald Williamson, a seventy year old executive, who was yet another powerful figure at NSC.

"Let me then explain in a much simpler fashion that you can understand. Do you know about numerology Mr. Williamson?" asked Jack.

"Yes, I do," replied Ronald.

"It applies to Earth's future as well, and through my calculation, the change in temperature and sudden catastrophic events occurring around the globe, suggest that a greater and a higher kind of magnetic pull is beginning to emerge. It's due to the fact that our solar system is reaching for a galactic plan of our galaxy, and will finally enter at 0:00:01 degrees on December 21st 2010, after which, there will be chaotic events around the globe. This entrance into the plain will increase the gravitational influence of each planet including the sun, which will begin attracting objects at a much faster speed including this mysterious planetary body.

Mayans believed that each pull in this galactic horizon was a dark rift, where each planet in our solar system will begin attracting other planets to itself, including the sun. This is what's know as change of energy, because Earth is a biological organism through my studies, and receiving this energy will change not only Earth, but humans beings to something which I do not know. If this planet is a living organism, we humans and animals are it cells."

"So, what is it that you're asking us to do Jack?" said Karen, who wasn't too thrilled to hear about Jack's nonsense, but showed some curiosity within her.

"Well, now that's up to you guys. What you want to do with this information and how you want to prepare for this project. I can't really give you any insight whether this planet will have any kind of intelligent life, or if they will be hostile. If you ask me, I would suggest that we build some sort of shield or defense system on the moon, just in case; because our technology won't be ready to handle the dark rift of the galaxy for the next billion years. I guess we should just do the best we can," said Jack.

"So, how much will this 'just-in-case' cost us?" asked Karen.

Jack stepped away for a moment, bowing his head and scanning the ground with his two eager eyes, he suddenly answered.

"65.1 billion dollars give-&-take," Jack replied.

All twelve board members burst-out into laughter, looking at each other while Jack held his eyes with two fingers in frustration and began erasing the equations from the chalkboard.

One of the board members whispered into Karen's ears, "How's his mental condition?"

"Don't worry, he's harmless. He has always been the strange one, and, he might be going through a divorce," replied Karen.

"Mr. Crawford," said Karen as Jack turned around.

"Yes," replied Jack.

"In your five years with NSC, have you researched any non-fictional problems beside your first project on the rover?" asked Karen.

"Non-fictional problems, gee that's a grand way of putting things together," said Jack.

"Have you Jack? Besides the ingenious work you did in developing the CPU for Mars rover," Karen asked in a most straightforward tone. Jack stared at her with arrogance, and then forced himself to answer, "Yes, I have."

"And what is that?" asked Ronald.

"I hope this doesn't turn out to be fictional hogwash, given the fundamental premise for an institution like NSC, is one that leans on such kind of boggling issues. Though I have not entirely completed the research, I might have a solution for guaranteeing a safe entry for the astronauts, when penetrating the atmosphere," said Jack.

"Alright, now that's a start, so what is it?" asked Karen.

"An enormous diamond," replied Jack.

"Lord...," whispered Karen. "What do you mean, Mr. Crawford?" Karen asked.

"The entire outer layer of the ship needs to be built of diamonds instead of ceramic tiles," replied Jack.

Out of frustration, Karen put her hand on forehead, "How much longer were you going to keep doing this research?" she asked.

"About four more years, I think," Jack replied.

"Four more years and three hundred thousand dollars per year to be exact, am I right Mr. Crawford?" stated Karen.

"That's okay, I can work on minimum wage if you wish," replied Jack with solid expression.

Jack cleared his desk, dumping all the important paperwork and files into a box which was already filled with photo frames, folders, and a pocket television. Kelly stood beside the wall, emotionally watching Jack pack up.

Karen walked in bewilderment asking, "What are you doing Jack?"

"I am just taking the initiative of doing something long before I am approached to do so," he replied.

"You're not getting fired, at least not at this moment." Karen glances over to Kelly, Jack's secretary. She realized the nature of the conversation and walked out of office, permitting the two individuals privacy.

Karen came near the desk, "You're one of the most brilliant minds here. You graduated from M.I.T with honors, received a presidential achievement award, and someone who attained a Ph.D. at a very young age. For crying out loud, do something with your life Jack. They can definitely use a creative genius like you in the Delta-23 project, and I can approach Graff about this if you like, or you could build a better telescope instead of wasting your precious time over E.T. and other fictional issues, like gemstones on a spacecraft and numerology. What the hell is wrong with you? What is this lunacy? If this is about Tracy, then take time off."

By now Jack had put all his belongings in the box. Storming out of the office, he stopped next to Karen to exclaim, "The roadway to truth is sometimes a dirty one. And I am willing to take it."

CHAPTER 3

JACK IN THE BOX

The sun shined radiantly on an area in Pennsylvania where an enormously deep hole was being dug for a new hotel. About forty construction workers were busy drilling and digging a huge deep hole in the ground. Above it, there were numerous other construction workers gathered near a lunch area devouring their food. Amongst a group of five construction workers was Jack Crawford, eating a greasy Philly cheese steak sandwich. His face and attire was covered in dirt. He seemed to be minding his own business while sitting with the rest of the men who were eating and talking.

Suddenly, a very jovial Bill softly taps Jack on the stomach. "Hey Jack, you heard about that new space convention happenin' in downtown tomorrow night?"

"Yeah, been there the past five years and it's the same old stuff and the same old toys I made, they never seem to change," replied Jack.

A third man who was intrigued by his answer asked, "What do you mean your toys?"

"What? You didn't know about our NSC genius, who left a great job to be with this gang of admirable dirt engineers," replied Bill.

"What's your story?" said the third man curiously.

"It's all crap, you guys may be fat and sloppy, but you're sure as hell far more trustworthy than any of those pricks up in Pasadena and Houston," Jack replied. He got up from his table, wiped his hands, and threw away the crammed bag containing his food and soda can. "Gentlemen, see you downstairs," said Jack as he walked away. The third guy not getting any of the gibberish that was just spoken to him by Jack, asked Bill for more clarification. "What's he all about?"

"He worked with NSC for about frive years, and never complained, minded his own business, helped develop the C.P.U. for the Mars rover, but when he told them about a possible alien planet coming towards earth, they thought he was crazy and fired him," replied Bill.

"So, how did he know about this planet?" The man asked.

"Well, it's his math mumbo jumbo that tells when a a planet-&-stuff should be arriving here. And it has something to do with astrology and numerology, who knows."

"What do you mean? This is confusing man," said the third man.

"The God damn Roswell crap they picked up in the 50s that's what it's all about. He believed they were just front line coming in and checking things before the entire army comes over. And so, after getting booted from practically every space program on this planet, he stopped believing in his passion and thought there was more peace in doing something like this. A place where he wouldn't be betrayed, or questioned for his unorthodox intelligence; leaving behind good money, nice cars and a beautiful ex wife."

"So much for having your own opinion, yeah, welcome to America," said the third man.

"Then who are those two kids that hang around him all the time? Are they his?" asked the fourth construction worker who was sitting right next to Bill.

"He adopted them from a homeless man, who was practically dying from cancer on the street. Jack didn't have the heart to walk away after seeing Michael and Lisa begging for food at only two years of age. I've never come across a man who defined the meaning of being a "Man", more than Crawford himself," replied Bill.

Jack finished up his shift, cleaned his hands and face and headed to the parking lot. Most of the SUV's and trucks were parked on the lot, while the rest of the workers were getting ready to leave. Jack went up to his truck and threw his dirty black towel in the back, opened the door and jumped inside. Just as he was about to take-off, Bill's truck came to a halt beside Jack's. "Hey Jack, you're coming down to the bar?" asked Bill.

"Is it taco Tuesday?" asked Jack.

"You're damn right, it is, and the Sixers are playing the Lakers," said Bill.

"Alright then, let's party," Jack replied.

"Are you going to pick up Michael and Lisa?" Bill asked.

"No, not right now, they won't be off from school before five thirty anyway," replied Jack.

Charlie's Pub, the board read on top of the bar, and the usual crowd had gathered inside. Truck drivers, bikers, young adults, and loud country music played in surround sound; as lights were dimmed-out everywhere, except around the pool table.

Jack and his crowd came and sat on the bar stools and ordered their drinks.

"So, will it be your usual? Jack black the NSC man," asked the bartender.

"Naa..., make it a JPL tonight," replied Jack.

"What about you boss?" the bartender asked Bill.

"Give me a pitcher of Rucker, will ya?" said Bill.

"One JPL and Rucker coming right up!" replied the bartender.

The bartender turned around and whispered, "Jack, she's on tonight's shift."

"Thanks for letting me know. I'll keep my eyes open," Jack replied with a blink.

Laura, whose face wasn't visible, was talking to someone on a cell phone in the back. She eagerly wanted to get off. It wasn't a pleasant conversation at all. It felt like she was trying to stop someone from calling her.

"I don't need you to be calling me anymore. I don't want anything to do with you. Do you get that? If you call me again, I swear I'll blow your horn," said Laura, as she hung up and left.

A beautiful girl with long black hair, stunning Italian looks came out from back wearing a snug tight black top with jeans and a black-banded wristwatch.

Laura was about to walk away but quickly glanced over with her big green-eyes and spotted Jack sitting in the corner. The young lady walked right in front of the table and made him a shot of the most expensive scotch on the counter.

"This one's on the house doctor," said Laura, while Jack looked at her with a soft impish smile and replied, "thanks, I thought you're off on Tuesdays."

"You know I began my seven-&-a-half year Saturn transit," said Laura while pouring one shot for herself.

"Good, I told you it'll be luck for you, it'll take you to new heights, just wear the Blue Sapphire ring on the middle finger," replied Jack.

Laura on the other hand already had one, and showed Jack the 'birdie'. "Great, thank you," replied Jack.

"How were the finals?" Jack asked Laura.

"I passed, but I see someone here didn't want to pick up my calls," said Laura.

"When did you call?" Jack asked with all curiosity.

"Wednesday night. I wanted to thank you by taking you and the kids out for dinner."

"Actually I took Michael and Lisa for bowling that night, and I must've left my cell in the truck, sorry about that."

"Really, was it Central Bowling park?" asked Laura.

"Yeah, the new place that just opened down the street."

"I was there all night on Wednesday, Jack! And I didn't see you anywhere."

Jack took a deep breath and picked up the shot of glass and took it all down.

"I guess this drink must have been my tuition fee then?" Jack told Laura. He looked at his watch and became restless. "Look at the time. I have to go pick up the kids; thanks for the drink. I needed it."

Just as Jack opened the door to his truck, Laura shut it no sooner. "What is it with you huh? Why do you play these games with me? Why don't you want to talk to me? Or maybe this is a NSC thing to get a girl all excited and then blast off into space without giving a cent of attention to her," Laura questioned.

"Laura. You're no doubt the most beautiful woman in this city and perhaps even the state. And I bet, outside of me, any handsome, decent, educated and wealthy man would love to be with you. But you've got to trust me on this one, wasting your life over a guy like me will not get you anywhere. You're young, beautiful and smart, so finish your school and become who you need to be. Believe me;

you don't want to be with a guy like me, no siree!" said Jack as he threw his jacket in the back of the truck.

"I am about this close to punching you in the stomach right now," said Laura.

"Hey, what did I do now?" Jack quickly asked.

"That's just it; you never do anything, that's the problem," Laura replied.

Jack glanced at one spot on ground for a while as he kept gazing back and forth at Laura. He played around with his foot on the dusty ground and spoke, "have you ever spent three days with me in my house? Have you ever seen the conditions in which I live in?" asked Jack.

"I really don't care about that," said Laura.

"Is that so? Well then, what are you up to for the next three days?" Jack asked swiftly.

"After tonight I'm off for the next three days."

"In that case bring at least three pair of clothing for change, a shampoo because I use the eighty nine cents one, and a clean brush because personally you do not want to use anything in my bathroom; you know where I live," said Jack without hesitation.

"I will. But can you tell me what is this all about?" asked Laura.

"You'll stay with me for three days and if you are content with what you see; I'll gladly love to be in a relationship with you, again," said Jack, who knew she wouldn't go for such a deal. But deep down inside he longed for her admiration. He was just afraid of give his heart to a woman again for fear of another shattered and broken heart.

"Gosh, I think that's a little too fast for me to make such a major decision again, especially knowing it's you. I want to be in your life, but, I want to do it at a normal pace, " Laura replied stepping backward.

"Hey honey, either it's all or nothing with me. Listen, dating you was an amazing time, but you know of my situation. No woman can stand my life, and, I've really never been good with people. Moon in the twelfth house, remember," said Jack.

"Don't give me your financial situation pep talk, I've never asked you for anything," replied Laura.

"Do you love me, honestly?" asked Jack.

"I want to, if you give me a chance," replied Laura.

"Then you're getting your chance," Jack answered.

They looked at each other for a while. Then, Jack sat in the truck and started the engine and began rolling away slowly. Laura spoke out as the truck was about to take speed. "Jack!" she shouted.

The truck stopped briefly as Jack looked back at her.

"I really do want to love you," said Laura.

Jack began to think, while looking down at the ground. He halted his truck, parked, jumped-out and headed towards Laura, holding her face in his hands he kissed her on the forehead.

"I hope these next three days will make you realize certain things about reality and fiction," said Jack.

He smiled and got back inside and drove off as she watched him leave.

Across the street from 17th Avenue a man in a gray jump suit walked across two buildings with a mop-bucket. From the side Jack appeared with his two children, Michael and Lisa. As they were walking, all three of them were engaged in a conversation about their day at school.

"And…and the fifth chapter, we read about Jupiter and Saturn. Our teacher said that one day the ring will disappear from Saturn and fall on earth," said Jack's adopted son Michael.

"No, she didn't. She said those rocks would fall back into Saturn after millions of years," interrupted Lisa, Jack's seven year old adopted daughter.

"That's right; they will fall back into Saturn. Were you playing paper soccer with Josh again during science class?" asked Jack.

"No, I was playing paper football with him today," Michael replied.

"Oh, that's a lot better than paper soccer I suppose?" said jovial Jack while walking.

All three of them got in the truck as Jack threw their backpacks in the back.

"What's for dinner dad?" asked Michael.

"Well, I was thinking maybe the three of us can cook together tonight."

"Okay soldiers, buckle up!" Truck's engine started as they drove off from the parking lot.

The snipped heads of dead fish were placed before layers of onion and other vegetables on a shining brown plate.

Whenever a fish's head was separated from its body, the cheering of Michael and Lisa could be heard in the background, as they both jumped with their hands in the air. Meanwhile Jack was unable to control his mirth, while wearing a dirty white apron.

"Okay, what do we cut next?"

"The tail," yelled Michael and Lisa at same time.

Jack quickly slammed the knife down on the fish, "and there goes the tail," said Jack. He then turned around and looked at the kids with an irritated face.

"Hey, what happened to my salad my junior chefs? Everything is on the dining table, and, unwashed," said Jack.

"Okay, we're on it chief," replied Lisa as both of them left the kitchen, while Jack cooked the fish. Pieces of marinated fish got dipped in a pan full of hot oil, which landed on Jack's hand and face, as he felt a quick sting and jumped back. "Outch…!" screamed Jack as he slammed the towel from his shoulder on the slab.

Jack came out of the kitchen with a bowl filled with fried fish and sat it on the dining table, where the two kids had decorated the table with salad, mashed potatoes, peas, a jug filled with coke and a plate filled with steamed rice.

The house was average with no particular decor.

Most of the stuff in the dining room was thrown around or shoved into spaces, and it seemed as though the place had never been properly cleaned. The room was lit from a dimmed orange light that was part of a ceiling fan. The table-top was made of a really cheap material cloth. Jack took off his apron and put it on top of the chair. "Okay troops, attack." As all three of them started digging, a loud knock frightened the excited family. Jack was caught by surprise, as a piece of fish flew from his hand.

He walked up to the door and opened it. He was startled by an unexpected surprise. Laura stood on the doorstep with a suitcase in her hand, and a smile that could knock the socks off any man.

"I thought I'd get an early start," said Laura, as she was eager to spend the next three days with Jack and his kids.

"You're really serious about this? I thought you would shrug it off like my other eccentric analysis on our friendship."

"Mmm…I smell fish," said Laura, ignoring Jack's question.

"I never thought you would even, I mean you're really serious, aren't you?"

"I'm really hungry, so are we having fish for dinner?"

Jack in a composed fashion invited her inside, "Yeah sure, come on in."

They both walked together inside the house as Laura put her small suitcase in the corner. Lisa saw her; she got up from her chair and ran right towards Laura.

"Laura, are you going to eat dinner with us?" asked Lisa excitedly.

Laura couldn't help but place a gentle smile on her face while picking up Lisa in her arms.

"Oh I am not just going to eat dinner; I'll be staying over night with you guys."

"What? Is this true dad?"

Jack glanced towards Laura and replied, "Yes, she is."

Michael, too, ran and grabbed Laura by her leg and wrapped himself around.

"Oh boy, you're getting pretty heavy Michael."

"I missed you sooo….much," said Michael.

Meanwhile, Jack stood on side, and observed the beautiful scene, and knew how attached these kids were to Laura.

She glanced up to Jack and gave an expression of devotion to Jack and his family.

"Okay, I don't know about you two but I am extremely hungry," said Laura as she walked over to dinning table while Michael hung onto her leg. She walked as if she was crippled; dragging Michael with her.

"Look, we made fish, mashed potatoes and rice for you," replied Lisa.

The children along with Laura started devouring the food, while Jack walked slowly towards the kitchen, observing his children finding a new meaning of happiness, wrapped up with feminine affection. As Laura ate, she glanced at Jack's direction asking, "Aren't you going to eat?"

"I think I'm full," replied Jack with a gentle smile on his face as he leaned against the wall with his arms folded.

"Dad, come on, let's eat," Michael shouted enthusiastically. Thereafter, Jack gradually walked over and sat down with Laura and kids. The atmosphere changed completely giving off a vibe of a happy, normal American home. The dining room had a new life and light to its ambience.

Stars twinkled brightly in the night sky as Laura's eyes gazed at them through a telescope. She stood behind a black sheet on Jack's porch. It was fairly cold outside, but even Laura couldn't keep her eyes off the universe when given the chance to glance.

"So, the one right next to that triangle is the closest star to Earth?" asked Laura.

"Well, after the Sun, yes," replied Jack, who stood next to her with his arms folded.

"Gosh, this thing is just as powerful as one we saw at the downtown science exhibition last year."

"Actually, it's a whole lot better since I've added 26 layers of optical lenses and 180 mirrors made by your very own."

"So why is it that a person with a Ph.D. in mathematics, previously working for one of biggest space agencies in the world suddenly becomes a construction worker? Never quite figured that one out," stated Laura.

"For peace of mind and some freedom, I guess." Jack seemed absorbed in his own world; he clearly had the tension and worries of a low-income single parent. He did however show determination and confidence, but he seemed to be a little more fragile with Laura around.

"I still can't believe how much those kids have gotten attached to you; considering you've only met them no more than eight times," said Jack.

"Well, I did take them to the city-fair that one time when you had to leave for some work emergency, remember," replied Laura.

"Really, when was this?" inquired Jack.

"You called me, just last month, when you had to do a graveyard shift, hello...." said Laura.

"I didn't know they went to the fair with you." Jack slowed his pace of conversation down. He started gazing into her eyes, trying to figure out, who this fictional woman is? That came into his life a couple of years ago and became intent to his world. "I also can't believe that you actually showed up, I mean here you are standing next to me, in my house, in middle of the night. I don't know, but I am scared."

"Did you ever think about why I like you so much Jack?" asked Laura.

"I know it has to be more than just my good-looks and charm, right? And I imagine you're not drawn to me because of my lucrative career as a construction worker, who's making less than thirty five hundred a month, so what is it then?" Jack asked.

"Well, it's definitely not because of the fact that you're the first man I know who loves kids so much that he adopted them, even as a single man. And I absolutely couldn't care less that a man as good looking as you; doesn't take home a different woman each night. Nor does he fall asleep until his kids have done so, and I don't think I'll fall for a man who is so confident that he left one of the biggest organizations, because he didn't receive the respect he deserved. And last but not least, he's quite a good chef too."

"So, what is it then?" Jack asked once again.

"I don't know, but I'll tell you all about it on my third day here, okay."

Laura and Jack stared at each other for a few seconds while Jack blurted out, "You can't imagine how difficult it is for me not to reach forward and kiss you."

"Go ahead Jack, you know I won't mind."

"I'm scared, every single relationship which had a kiss involved, ended up breaking apart. God Laura, I wish you could've lived my life, only then a woman can understand this strangeness in my personality, this antisocialism with extreme passionate behavior, it can scare anyone off, even you. That's why I don't intend to ruin it."

Jack could feel what his soul-desired, and what his heart wanted. He had this beautiful woman standing in front of him, who not only loved him but cared for his kids like her own.

Taking a deep breath he slowly took Laura in his arms. She felt comforted and at peace while slowly resting her head on his chest. They didn't say a word to each other, but rather, had their heartbeats do the talking.

Jack sat on a wooden stool and stared at his blackboard with a mathematical equation in the middle of the night, perhaps early morning, but he didn't care. This was his passion and his curse. To blindly adore what he created, and sink himself like any other master of this Universe would. Jack stood up and took off the rest of the bed sheet that covered the board.

"What the..." said Laura softly as Jack quickly glanced back in panic and then settled down as he saw Laura standing behind in calm manner.

"This is a math problem," said Jack.

"Yeah, I see that," replied Laura.

"So you just haven't been sitting still all these years have you?" said Laura.

Jack pointed her to a small section of calculation on the board.

"See this. It took me eight months just to solve this part, then after that it was fairly easy to finish the rest. But I don't think it's accurate for some reason."

"What is this all about?" Laura asked Jack.

"This is about its arrival," replied Jack.

"Arrival of who?"

Jack was in total silence for a few seconds and then finally replied, "The dark planet."

"Nibiru?" asked Laura.

"Go ahead laugh, it doesn't bother me anymore," Jack told Laura.

"Do you hear me laughing?"

Jack turned around and looked at her, then turned back to the board. He walked over to the washing machine and picked up a black marker.

"You believe in numerology?" asked Jack.

"The birth number?" asked Laura.

Jack glances at Laura and said, "Yeah exactly."

"I know my life path is 8," replied Laura.

Jack became curious and said, "Are you? So am I."

Laura then told Jack as she slowly walked over to him, "Either we will be bankrupt or on top of the world, sometimes both."

Jack smiled and said, "Or getting fired for being stubborn and relentless, you might want to add."

"It's one of our good qualities, I think. Did you know that 70% of all CEOs in corporate America have 8 as their life path?" said Laura.

"And Scorpios," Jack put his two-cents into the conversation. He continued with his discussion while working on the board. "The study of numerology is 80% more accurate than rest of horoscopes you read about; because, everything in the Universe is made of numbers or based on numbers, which you can use to predict coming events of space and time. In reality whatever you see in the sky is merely the past. Vedic Astrology is another entity for predicting these things, but you need to be a good psychologist to predict through its matrix."

Jack started crunching and equating various numbers on board, while Laura listened attentively.

"Why are you so into celestial science?" asked Laura.

"I don't call it celestial science; I tend to call it celestial spirituality. My life just made more sense to me when I came across a numerologist, who perfectly explained my isolated personality and distant relations with everyone around me. He was so accurate in his prediction that I wondered if this planet is as alive as I am. I may be able to understand it more if I did a numerological calculation for it, and try to find out its past and what might happen in the future."

"It actually make sense, and not just spiritually," said Laura, who was blown away by jack's small and simple theory.

"The top scientists think that the Universe will collapse after 15 billion years, however, what they fail to realize is that a nursery of stars has been here for at least 118 billion years before the Universe was even formed."

"What nursery of stars?" asked Laura as she stepped forward into the dim light wanting to absorb all that Jack had to offer from his mysterious and genius brain.

"Well, it's a much bigger place than your brain can imagine that produces stars and galaxies. Although I don't exactly know how it all happens but I am aware that it's there, and it is producing stars million times bigger than our own Sun. Usually it happens where these giant gas storms curve up in little pockets of balls, and begin burning, creating fire, distribution, and the whole nine-yards."

"What about the faces on Mars and those so called pyramids?"

"They are there, and they do exist, not just from a conspiracy theorists view, but logically. The mountains on Cydonia Mars are shaped in what you call tetrahedron structure, which can only be built by a certain entity; not naturally. I saw those pictures the first time, before they were taken away from our entire team, and, were classified top secret. I was five minutes too late in scanning them. What you see on the internet is a manipulated version of the truth. They already discovered the same glass structure on the moon during the first landing. If you saw the movie 2001 Space Odyssey, It's really not far from the truth. I'm telling you this because, because, I don't know why but I just feel like taking this burden off my chest. Our kids in science class learn about the phases of the moon and why we only see one side in all the lands occupied by humans on Earth, and not the other side. I think there is a deeper reason, perhaps because they can keep a close eye on us from the biggest window in the sky. This is why NASA has never gone back to the moon; I don't think they got clearance from them."

"Them who?" asked Laura.

"Them' are the ones who may be watching us, studying us, and scrutinizing us, with envious eyes."

"So, what the heck are you doing wasting your life then? This is as good as career suicide," Laura stated abruptly.

"Now imagine what marrying me would be like. Are you seriously staying here, in my house for the next three days?"

"Oh yeah!" said Laura.

Jack had his face turned away from Laura, as he quietly whispered "Thank you..." He wanted to thank a higher entity for bringing such a stubborn woman into his life. A woman who wouldn't give up on him like other women did in his past, perhaps due to his unorthodox approach to life and relationships. But Laura was turning out to be different; she was turning out to be a mirror of him.

Laura's lips suddenly approached Jack's neck as she quickly turned him around and gave him a passionate kiss. The electricity felt like a supernova's explosion as Jack and Laura's lips communicated their desires.

"I'm going to sleep now," said Laura who slowly walked away and headed upstairs.

"What sleep?" said Jack to himself, as his eyes followed Laura's path. He knew, just from that one touch of her soft lips, his entire sleep had been stolen away.

CHAPTER 4
DISCOVERY

The sun rose above the farms of Philadelphia as morning birds spread their wings in cool air.

Trucks began to pull up in front of the construction site, where Jack was working, and five other men came down the elevator.

The sight manager signed every guy to a separate station to begin digging inside the deep hole. Jack got section 'A' again. He looked happy, and in high sprits, as Bill walked across.

"Did something special happen last night," said Bill.

"Something like that..." Jack replied with a smile.

"Alright lets rock-&-roll," said the site manager as he got up on an elevator.

Jack and everyone else in the pit started digging with tremendous tenacity. Jack used all his strength to keep up with his coworkers. The sun poured onto his head. Each pick of the shovel gathered a smooth layer of dirt, and the rhythm of the shovel made the process seem effortless.

Digging and digging, Jack kept plunging through. Suddenly, the rhythm of the shovel was interrupted. Jack had hit something hard in the ground. He dug the ground with his hands and saw a black metal object emerging from the ground. Carefully looking, Jack kneeled down and dug more avidly with his hands. The black metal started becoming more recognizable as Jack's curiosity continued to grow.

Curiously, Jack scanned around to see if anyone was looking, but they were all busy in their work. He discovered a small black box covered in dirt.

"Lunch truck is here!" yelled the site manager from the top, and within a matter of minutes more than 80% of the workforce stepped through an elevator, while Jack mindlessly sat over the black device.

"You coming Jack?" said Bill while heading towards the elevator.

"Yeah I just need to make a call, you guys go," Jack replied while pretending to make a call on his cell phone.

The moment he had a moment of privacy, Jack paid his full attention to the mysterious box, which, on further observation, was not a box at all. It was more like some device with a small screen in front; perhaps to tell time. His eyes opened wide and he started looking at the device. Turning it around and looking underneath, a small screen was blinking the word, "KYIRUX."

"Oh my God…" whispered Jack to himself.

He turned around in panic, and realized he was the only one left inside the foundation, while everyone else was on the ground level.

He picked the device up and headed for an elevator. He felt weird holding the device in his hand. He began to sweat, and started feeling a bit dizzy. He knew it wasn't just the bright Sun, but there was something within this mystic device that was changing the temperature within his body. It was perhaps an indication it was communicating with him in some telepathic manner, giving him a sense that it was alive and observing him.

Luckily there was no one around the area since the whole crowd was gathered in front of lunch truck. Jack calmly got out. He kept his eyes on the workers and knew that he had to act normal in order to sneak the device out in a huge pile of dirt.

"I am going to set the rollers in the 36 east direction and bring the T-D trucks on the west side," a line manger speaking to another senior engineer.

Jack walked up to him and tapped him on the shoulder.

"Hey Mark, can I talk to you for a second?" said Jack.

"Excuse me," said Mark to the engineer as he pulled himself away with Jack.

"What's up?"

"I think I have a fever, I was just wondering if Ben can do my section for the rest of the day."

"Hey don't worry, if you're sick you're sick, plus I am a week ahead in my schedule, so don't sweat it."

"Alright thank you," Jack replied with a sigh of relief.

Nodding his head Mark relieved Jack from his work. Jack slowly walked over to parking lot, pretending to have an upset stomach. Once inside the truck, he quickly raced off to the Main Street.

Jack, kicked opened the main door of his house while holding the device in his hands. Breathing heavily, he entered, closed the door, while peaking outside the side window. He came down to his basement and laid the black device on a tool table. For some time, he simply tried to catch his breath. Slowly his eyes refocused on the black device.

The sign of "KYIRUX" blinked rapidly. Jack just stared at it with a blank expression on his face and sat on the last step of the stairs.

The tube light in his basement began to flicker. He got up and nervously walked around the tool table with excitement in his body.

The black device spoke to Jack in a telepathic manner, it called out to him, almost begging him to explore it. Jack started observing the black box very carefully.

"Who are you?" whispered Jack nervously to the machine and gazed with passion and curiosity. He then glanced at the clock because it reminded him of something and proceeded to take out his cell phone and dial a number.

"Limburger Constructions, this is Jennifer."

"This is Jack Crawford; can I please speak to your site manger in department 112?"

"One moment sir…"

The lady transferred the phone call as it rang in Thomas' office.

"Thomas Anderson."

"Thomas this is Jack Crawford."

"Jack, my main man, what's going on brother? How is the fever?"

"Not too well, just need your help with something," replied Jack.

"Sure brother, speak."

"I'm on site 64, was anything here before?" asked Jack.

"What do you mean what was there before?" Thomas asked.

"Like, what was there before we started digging for the hotel?"

"Nothing, it was a pile of wasteland for the last, well, God knows how long," Thomas replied.

"There wasn't any electronic shop or military base of any sort right?"

"No, why are you asking?"

"Nothing, nothing at all, alright thanks a lot man," Jack ended the call as he questionably looked at the black device.

He started to feel doubt and concern in his head and it clearly showed on his face. He pondered for a while without blinking an eye. Jack rushed to one of his cabinets, where he started searching for something in a pile. He took out a small monitor with a black cable and laid it near the black box.

As he went towards the wall, he noticed a hanging bedsheet which was covering a secret locker. He opened it and brought out a briefcase. He laid it next to the small monitor, which was near the black box.

He took out some test tubes, bottles and a glass equipped device. After attaching them together, Jack plugged in the small monitor.

He opened up a bottle of green jelly liquid and poured it inside a test-tube. He then hooked the test-tube on a holder as various graphs appeared on the monitor.

After taking a small cotton ball and rubbing it gently on the black device, he proceeded to throw the cotton inside the tube containing green gel. He waited and watched.

The meter on the monitor started to move slowly as the cursor pulsed on the small screen. Various charts began to change their calculations and numberings.

The cursor kept pulsing as Jack's eyes were stuck on the screen. The numbers 000.500, 000,000.00 appeared. Jack's eyes couldn't believe the result. He picked up the small monitor and looked at it carefully.

Jack walked over to his desk in the corner and picked up one of the many rocks lying around the table, and with new cotton ball from the briefcase, rubbed it on its surface, then, threw it back inside test tube.

After a few seconds monitor showed 666.00, Jack quickly took new cotton out from the bag and again rubbed it on the black device, then dunked it into the liquid gel again.

Jack waited and watched for the third time. This time curser pulsed for a bit longer. The result showed 000.500, 000,000.00

"Can't be," whispered Jack to himself, as he didn't know what to think at the moment.

He put the black box in his secret locker and covered it back with bed sheet, quickly grabbed his jacket and rushed upstairs.

<u>Bucks County Community College</u>

Logan was dusting his cabinet.

His facial expressions and body motion revealed a secretive nature. After cleaning the glass on the top shelf of his cabinet, he stepped down from the step stool. His eyes glanced at the window for quick second, and noticed a figure running inside his building.

Glancing at the open window, Logan saw Jack running towards his classroom. He took out his glasses and walked towards the door.

"Logan! Need to talk to you," said Jack as he rushed inside his classroom, catching his breath.

"Jack, is that you?"

"Yeah, you got a minute to spare?"

"Yeah, what is it?"

"I need to borrow your ageist meter."

"What for?"

"I just found an old potter at my work and wanted to see if it was more than 500 hundred years old."

Logan softly laughed behind his desk. He opened the lights to the room, and walked over to Jack.

"You're becoming a paleontologist now?" asked Logan.

"Yes, something like that, you know me," Jack replied.

"I actually do know you. And no broken potter would get your eyes this bright, at least not for the man who invented the age detecting device. It must be something very old for you to confirm it twice and not trust your own work. Although I am not going to ask you what it is that you found, I am going to ask you to keep it away from the hands of those who would like to hide it from the public."

Jack, without speaking, followed Logan towards a blue double door.

"Your silence speaks louder than your words, to convince me it's not a pottery you found during your construction work, my old friend."

"Listen," said Jack as he held his shoulder "I will tell you once I figure it out, I am in a tight predicament right now," Jack replied.

"You don't need to figure it out, it will figure you out Jack," said Logan as he opened the doors to the science lab which contained all sorts of engineering devices on tables and shelves. They both meandered through to the end of the lab. Logan took his key out, and opened a locked cabinet. He took out a small device with two clamps and thick wires. The machinery was boxed in a transparent package.

"The class won't be using this for the entire semester," said Logan.

"Don't you worry, I'll bring this back today, I just need to confirm something for two seconds." replied Jack.

"Yeah, yeah, don't worry; it's an honor Dr. Jack."

"Your openness to lend your valuable hands to me, means a more than anything to me, even my own ambitions," said Jack, as he was very thankful for Logan's support.

"Your ambitions are a virtue to this world. It is an honor," Logan replied as he handed the device to Jack.

"I have a PhD in psychology from M.I.T, I am sure you're not aware of it, but through my experience I know you have the key to this world within your grasp," said Logan.

Jack quietly glanced at Logan then looked elsewhere and said, "It may be, but M.I.T? Then what are you doing here?"

Logan looked right into Jack's eyes, but didn't say a word. After a few moments of silence he spoke "Why aren't you at NSC Jack? What is a man like you doing construction work?"

"You know my reasons."

"Now you know my reasons," replied Logan, as Jack saw his own reflection in him.

"I have no means to send harm your way, by speaking of your ambitions to this world. I am the only one that knows who you are and I tend to keep it that way," said Logan.

"Thank you so much, I'll be back," Jack replied and walked quickly outside the classroom, then ran to the parking lot.

From the darkness light appeared, as Jack opened the door to his secret locker and pulled out the mysterious KYIRUX box.

Jack stared at it like an opponent on other side of the war field. He again walked around it slowly observing the object. The device was pure black with only KYIRUX repeatedly glowing. There was no avoiding it.

Jack set the age-detecting device right next to the tool table. He opened it up, and plugged all the things into proper sockets, and with the two clamps hanging, he attached them on both sides of the KYIRUX box.

After punching some numbers on the small keyboard, Jack constantly looked at the small screen. The object blinked a red light for about thirty seconds. He waited and watched the small little light. After it turned green Jack punched in a code again and watched.

On the screen it read 500,012,682. He slipped to the ground, shocked from the result. He was sitting on his bended knees, not knowing what to do next.

Slowly, he got up and came near the object again. Jack took the clamps off from each side and as soon as the right clamp detached from the object, a much-bellowed sound of a male echoed, "MINAASTINAA, OUMMNAA...."

Jack, visibly shaken, quickly jumped back while looking at the object. His head smashed into a wooden cabinet and he felt the pain in his head but didn't lose eye contact with the object.

From the look of Jack's eyes one could tell he was scared and paranoid. He could not understand what was happening in his world at the moment. He sat on the ground and rested his hands on the cabinet, while his fear gave way to keen anticipation.

The voice came back again, and echoed, "NIM MAYO HO BHRIM MAY KYO…"

Jack got up and hit his head again on the rack above. He tried to keep his eyes on the object, while managing the pain in his head.

Jack rubbed his thumb on the bright green screen that read "KYIRUX."

Suddenly, thoroughly having scared the hell-out of Jack, the abrupt sound faded. He got another sudden shock from this change in sound that he fell back on the ground and crawled to the last step of the stairs. He knew something was not right, and it might be too late to fix it. He knew his life had changed in the past 50 minutes.

A silver bright laser began to appear from both sides of KYIRUX and came together at a center point where it merged. It then gave birth to a third laser which was a bright green color almost like a beam which went across the top side of the box and into the back side.

Jack was getting nervous and panicky; tumbling across the room he watched this device doing all sorts of strange things.

Jack picked up a white bed sheet and threw it on the black box thinking it would stop. Questioning his own rather naïve move, Jack removed the bed sheet from the top of the device. The green laser had given this black box a very mechanical design.

White steam started to shoot out from both sides of this box, and then slowly the green outlined shape began to dissolve itself like cream in coffee. The core matter appeared from within, as the device opened itself.

Jack carefully looked onto this new mysterious machine which had a mind of its own, and just like the outer layer it had the glowing KYIRUX sign that was brightly lit inside.

"This can't be happening, what... and who are you?" said Jack. The light kept blinking without interruption.

The sound of rattling, opening and shutting doors could be heard upstairs. Dragging it to the corner Jack quickly put the bed sheet over the machine and ran upstairs. He stopped and controlled his emotions when he saw Laura standing in front of him. Laura stared at him suspiciously.

"You're already home?" asked Laura.

"Welcome home honey," Jack replied sarcastically, acting as though everything were completely normal.

"Kind of feels good to come home to someone who says that," said Laura while putting her bags down on the side.

"I can get use to it," Jack replied.

"Are you picking up the kids or I?" asked Jack.

"I was thinking both of us can," replied Laura. Jack looked towards the basement and then glanced back at Laura.

"Sure," Jack replied, looking at the basement door again.

Driving off in between the neighborhoods, Laura seemingly asked Jack a question.

"Why do you look a little different?" asked Laura.

"Different, I don't know, may be it had something to with last night."

"May be, but no, can't be."

"Why?" Jack asked Laura.

"Because I've kissed you before and you never seem to be so mystified the next day, except to call me to make a good argument about how selfish and self indulgent I am, and a girl like me only belongs in a bar not a house."

"But I did always apologize every evening on my second call, but I guess our kiss had something passionate about it for me to be acting like this," said Jack.

"How much total time have we spent with each other in the past two years?" Laura asked.

"Total time? As if you were to say 24/7, I would say about two weeks," Jack replied while he kept his eyes on the road.

"Don't you think it's enough for a cancer woman to know about what her guy is thinking? Who she looks after more than her own life sometimes," said Laura. Jack putting his both hands on each side of his cheeks, tried to resolve this mysterious issue in his head, but subconsciously replied to Laura's questions," You're amazing you know that, and thank you for being you," said Jack absent-mindedly. He stood silent for a few moments while in confusion. "I had an upset stomach so I took-off from work."

Laura drove quietly without saying a single word. She understood the delicacy of the moment, and didn't want to ruin it. Their car smoothly drove through the neighborhood, while the Sun was about to set.

The car pulled up in front of the school. Michael and Lisa were sitting with their teacher and four other kids who were also waiting for their parents. Laura honked and waved her hand to the kids.

Anxiously the teacher asked Lisa.

"Is she your mom?"

Lisa glances at Michael and then looked at the teacher in the eye.

"No, but I think she'll make one of the best ones."

They both ran towards the car as Laura got out and hugged them in her arms like any biological mother would. Jack was speechless and again didn't want to interrupt the moment he was witnessing. The confusion of the entire day seemed to have taken a backseat to Laura and kids.

Back on the dining table, all four of them were eating Italian food while Laura stared at Jack, perhaps waiting for a reaction or a gesture from him.

"It's good, it's really good, I love it, you're a good cook," said Jack.

"Laura can you move in with us?" said Michael in excitement while Jack choked on the food. Laura laughed while Jack gulped the whole glass of water down in one go.

"Yes, she should live with us dad, can we keep her please…"

Laura pleads to Jack with the kids.

"Yes please dad," Laura giggled.

"Ok, you kids haven't been getting a lot of sleep, so finish your food fast and head to bed." Jack wanted to smile and say yes but something just held his answer on the lips.

"You're washing the dishes right?" Jack asked Laura as he got up from the table and went inside the kitchen.

"Sorry we're going to bed," replied Laura.

"Good," said Jack as he went into the kitchen to put his plate in the sink, he came back and took the plates of his kids while they were almost finishing up with dinner.

"Why are you in such a hurry?" Laura questions him as she looks a little angry.

"Are you done with your plate?" Jack quickly asked.

"No, I am not, and don't you dare touch my plate."

"Why did I even ask?" replied Jack sarcastically.

He went back into the kitchen, threw all the dishes in the sink, and quickly came back out. He picked up his kids and took them to their room.

"Can we watch T.V?" asked Lisa.

Jack stopped and quickly did some thinking, "ahh… sure, but, only for 30 minutes and then off to sleep. Are you done with your plate?" Jack asked Laura once again as he rushed back to the dining room.

"I think you need more sleep than them," replied Laura.

Laura stormed behind him and turned him around from the shoulder.

"What is it that you're hiding?"

"Hiding…? Nothing…"

"What are you hiding? Before I get out from you the old Chicago way," she said with her big angry eyes.

Jack halted himself and took Laura by her shoulders.

"You're going to have to wait till they are asleep, but yes, there is something in this house."

Laura looked into his eye for few seconds, rushed out of the kitchen and into the kid's room.

"Ok who wants to hear a bed time story?"

"I do," exclaimed Michael and Lisa at the same time.

"Ok come on, get on the bed," said Laura as she picked Michael with her left hand and laid him on the bed.

Night fell into the eyes of the children as they slept worriless in Laura's arms. The door to the room opened slowly as Jack peaked inside. Laura noticed him and slowly took her hands out from underneath Michael and Lisa.

Jack felt a teardrop slide down his eye, but before Laura could notice it, he quickly wiped it away. As Laura walked slowly out of the room, Jack shocks her with an incredibly passionate kiss, something she has never felt before.

"Ok who the hell are you and what did you do with Jack?" said Laura looking into Jack's eyes.

"The hell with him, he's dead, plus I am much better looking."

"Ok, it's still you," said Laura as she smiled at Jack.

"I am not going to say it, not right now," Jack whispered into Laura's ear.

"You don't have to."

Looking straight into her eye Jack promised to Laura, "I'll change my life as of now."

"You don't have to. Really," said Laura as she moved her hands through his hair, and in one crystallized moment, they fell in love.

"Can you promise me something right now?" asked Jack, as he changed the tone and expression on his face.

"What?" Laura asked Jack.

"Whatever I am about to show you will only stay between you and I, and no one else."

"Look in my eyes, what gave you that doubt?" replied Laura.

"Come with me," said Jack as he grabbed her hand and took Laura into the basement.

Lights opened, as the tube flickered more than usual, the buzzing sound of the light was heard in the quiet basement.

"Ok, you may not be able to understand what this is, but making a pre-judgmental theory would be the wrong way to go," Jack told Laura.

Nodding her head, Laura didn't say a word but was curious to find out what he had in the magic box. Jack walked over to the tool trolley and brought it to the middle of the floor as the bed sheet covered it.

"Looks like an engine to a Ferrari," Laura whispered.

"It's a little more advanced than that, or I think so," replied Jack.

Jack removed the bed sheet from the table.

"KYIRUX" she said to Jack, as she read the pulsating sign.

The sign was still slowly fading in & out on the screen.

"What the hell is it, a bomb?" Laura asked Jack.

"Can't be, you and I are still here.

"I really haven't explored it; I found it today at work, it was buried in the ground."

Laura being curious brought her hand over the flat plate of the device; suddenly a dark blue keyboard appeared from underneath the device.

"Wo..wo…I didn't know it could do that." Jack said to Laura.

"It looks like some sort of a computer," she replied.

"Alright let's see what these keys can do," said Laura.

Her finger slowly hovered over to the biggest button on the keyboard. Without pressing on the button it automatically recognized her finger and compressed itself. Quickly from the side, three lasers lights appeared in different color, Red, Green and Blue, and morphed into an outline of a huge monitor.

"Ok. What did I just do?" said Laura as she panicked and moved back with Jack.

Jack with his big blue eyes looked at the lit button; he took his hand over the keyboard as the symbols changed again. This time they converted into mathematical symbols.

"wha …wha ..wha … what the hell just happened?" said Jack, as he tried to figure out the changes in the keyboard. "Put your hand over this thing again," said Jack.

Her hand came over, and the keys again changed into the previous symbols.

"Do you know what these symbols are?" asked Jack.

"Yeah, they are Holy Jewish symbols, why?" replied Laura.

"You're Jewish?" asked Jack in shock.

"You got a problem with that?" asked Laura with anger.

"No, not at all; makes this thing a whole lot easier for me now."

"I think these keys change to what an individual can understand to the best to their ability, according to their knowledge base," Laura said.

"And you understand Hebrew better than English?" asked Jack sarcastically.

"You seem to have a problem with me and my being Jewish, don't you?"

"No…. I was just curious to know why the keys would change like that?"

Jack's hand slowly moved towards the keys, as they changed their symbols again. "Wait", Laura warned Jack.

"What?"

"May be it's a bomb or something."

"It's not, I know."

Laura went over to the washing machine and picked up an empty plastic bucket, came and stood behind Jack.

"Okay, go-ahead," said Laura.

Jack turned around with a confused face and nodded his head; he was really mesmerized by Laura's humor. Jack got himself together and glanced at the keyboard.

"Must be that Jewish humor," whispered Jack to himself.

"Ok, I will have to see which button to touch first," said Jack.

Jack scanned the keyboard and saw the symbol of infinity lit. He brought his finger on top of the key and got very close to the button. The symbol transformed into the color red. Sweat dripped from the sideburns on Jack's face; blinking his eye rapidly and taking a deep breath he pressed the button. He and Laura kept looking at the button as though nothing was going to happen. Then a round sphere appeared from the middle of the keyboard, it was a sea compass, which was slowly rotating. The laser started to flicker brighter and brighter, while Jack and Laura started to crawl back without removing their gaze from the machine. Both sat on the bottom step of the stairs, she put her hands around Jack and held him tight by the shoulder.

Small blue lights popped up around the compass and suddenly a bright white screen exploded from the lasers and surrounded Laura and Jack. Both of them hid their eyes from the light and ducked for cover. After a few moments they slowly opened their arms with squinting eyes. The whiteness started to fade out as the screen dimmed and a figure began to appear.

The astronaut stood in front of beautiful sunset that was disappearing behind the icy mountain. Jack and Laura stared while not a single hair moved on their body. Behind the astronaut, three other alien astronauts came walking in different color suits towards him. They reached him and opened their helmets. Two females; Anathema and Lava with a male astronaut whose name was Calculus, stared at the setting Sun without blinking their eyes.

"I could've killed one of you to see this," said the first astronaut to his collogues referring to the beautiful setting Sun.

"I would've too sir," replied Calculus.

"You were going to kill me?" Anathema asked with her angry eyes.

"Oh no, just Lava and the captain, then we would've taken over the ship. Like the plan?" replied Calculus.

"Are we camping out then captain?" asked Lava to the first astronaut while he didn't move his eyes from the Sun.

Looking straight into the setting sun, the astronaut replied, "yes, this is home for now." Lava turned around and walked back to the ship.

Anathema reached into her left jacket pocket and took out a silver glowing tube, and handed it to her captain. He took the tube in front of his face and pressed a button. Two bright lights pop out from each sides of this silver cylinder with a tiny lens. He brought the device in front of him, looking directly into it, and spoke.

"My name is Pascal. I am the caption of the ship SYIRUX-82. We are currently at the edge of our galaxy Nebula Oxford located in 46.41-556 degree on the north horizon, and have landed on the third planet of a 12 planetary system now ageing 8.7 billion years, and to die off in the next 16.37 billion years. Our mission is to reach White Gates. I and 120 other astronauts have made the decision not to return back to our star system in our lifetime, but to explore this Universe and send the information back to our Planet Divya-82 and other celestial bodies with intelligent life. Our job and passion is to explore, and to come in peace with every single life form that exists in this dimension.

"I shall give the rest of the report soon."

The camera on the pen turned off as well as the light of the KYIRUX computer. Astonished Jack and Laura stared at each other in middle of the dark basement. Jack took a step forward and looked back at Laura, who took two steps back while she held her heart.

Jack had won the lottery, that's what he was thinking, and without communicating with Laura, they both knew that the Universe was talking to them, its soul had heard Jack's call, and answered him in a single defining moment.

It was so quiet in the basement, that both a pin drop and the creepy crawling of a spider could easily be heard. Jack tightly gripped his hair with both hands, while his eyes began to grow large from the rattling words of Pascal.

"What do you want to do?" Laura asked.

"Oh my God, what just happened?" Jack replied.

"You weren't really sick were you?"

"I can't believe you're still asking that question."

"Is this really true, and if it is, it's already changed everything in the science books," said Laura.

"Do you want to look at it again?" asked Laura.

"Hell yeah," replied Jack.

Lisa walked in the basement while rubbing her eyes. "Dad what's going on?" Jack and Laura turned around quickly and reached up to Lisa.

"Oh sweetie, dad and I heard a big cat inside the basement jumping off of the washing machine, so we came down to check it. Come here, I'll put you to bed."

Jack kept looking at the computer. Laura picked Lisa up and walked upstairs. Jack sat down and without hesitation pressed on a different button. This time nothing happens but the entire keyboard turns green while only one button turns red. Jack glances and presses the red button quickly. Again the RGB lights flicker and the screen appears again. This time it was inside the spaceship as Jack watched closely.

"Oh my God," said Jack while watching. Pascal came back online and continued his video journal.

"Welcome to chapter 2 of our odyssey, where I'll show you the current condition of our ship and the energy resources we've used for the last 757.5 light years. I know it's impossible for us to be alive after such a long time, but our ship is traveling at 3.2 light years every 500 days. And we have used event-horizon quite often, which I'll explain later in this video guide."

"Going faster than the speed of light was impossible in the past. We thought our bodies weren't ready for such speed, and we also discussed the aging process while traveling. Nothing changed. Our bodies remain the same and the people we left, remain the same in our test runs. We don't know; it's a matrix we haven't figured out. The speed was achievable by using laser beam for throttle with Septon molecules. The architect to this technology will be available as a blueprint inside the KYIRUX device you possess."

Pascal walked inside the control room network while explaining each section that he visited. "This is the main network resource deck. It automatically evaluates the direction of the ship; wherever life is forming where planets are present. We have also compiled detailed formats and components of 300,000 different gasses and compounds we found in our way. Diamonds cover the outer layer of our ship, it's the second hardest material that we found on our own planet, the number one material was "Mannai", and it's found in the mouth of one of the reptilians on Divya-82. It's quite unique to find such material inside a living thing, welcome to this Universe. That's the best way I can explain these phenomenon."

"Our outer layer helps us penetrate though any kind of thick or dense atmosphere without doing any damage to the ship."

Pascal walked forward into the hallway and reached the colorful wall where billions of different currents and circuits were in work. A robot that was manufactured by Pascal and his team of scientist was working inside. "She is ZELTA 2 our meteorologist. She is in-charge of gathering all the weather and climate information for a particular body we have interest in landing on." ZELTA looked into the camera and bowed her head in respect.

Pascal exited the room and walked through the white hallway towards a dead-end. Nearing the wall, he suddenly took a left; a giant football sized open space lay in the middle of the ship. It was an area where other aliens like him, were working on very unique machines. It looked nothing like the machinery or computers on Earth in current times; everything was white including their outfits.

"We have used the color white for many of our necessities and accessories, due to the fact its helps the brain think more clearly in a stressful situation, and calms us down during a panic hour. Color therapy is one of the most important medications on our planet."

Pascal, without any safety, stepped on to the edges, which lead 50 feet down on to the ground. But while putting his first step forward, a plate automatically came up and held Pascal's feet and brought him down.

Lava rushed out from one of the rooms and walked on the floor where Pascal was walking. "Captain we may have a little problem," said Lava.

"What is it?" Pascal asked calmly.

"I think you better come with me," replied Lava.

Following Lava, he walked in a calm and peaceful manner, while smiling and saluting to working scientists on the floor. "Apparently one of the cages malfunctioned inside the dome, as four male Ginks were found in the female Ginks cages," explained Lava.

"Any fatalities?" Pascal asked.

"No captain, it's the complete opposite."

The door to the back corridor opened. In the white cages were about 4 male chimpanzee looking creatures sitting with a female version. Sitting beside them were 5 little baby chimpacreatures.

"When was their last checkup?" asked Pascal.

"I am guessing about nine weeks ago," replied Lava.

"Why was this department neglected?"

"They get timely supply of food, water, medicine and full body checkup ever 3 weeks by SYIRUX 11," Lava replied.

"Why didn't the alarms go off?" asked Pascal.

"I am sorry sir but this section never had an alarm, these animals were put here at the last two hours of our departure. It was your call."

"I see," Pascal replied and walked out of the room.

"So what do you want to do captain?" Lava asked.

"There might be a way, let me finish the video session, meanwhile, secure the cages, and have the babies checked."

"Yes captain."

Pascal walked away and continued his video journal tour. He stepped inside a huge room with thousands and thousands of small shelves, which were lit with fluorescent lights.

"This is our nutrition vault, it stores every kind of vitamin, mineral, and protein that is required for survival. Although we do stop from time to time on different planets to gather native resources till the vault is full."

He punched a password on the wall as all the red and green sections opened up. On the trays were toothpaste like tubes with an animated logo and symbols on them. At least 40% of the trays were empty. He picked one of the tubs up and brought it close to the pen.

"This one tube can last a single person 2.5 years. Just a drop of it will fill a grown Divyan's stomach. As you might have noticed we are running out of them, this is why we have made a stop on this planet."

Pascal turned around in concern as Lava stood at the door way.

"I will take care of the ginks, not to worry," said Pascal.

"I don't think the ginks are the only problem, Boxter 6 found a mysterious gas in the atmosphere."

Pascal looked into the camera.

"I shall return in a moment."

The computer got shut-off but Jack didn't stay still. He scanned his hand over the keyboard again. The keyboard sparked a light a few times and then died. A small liquid meter appeared and showed a glowing green liquid towards the end. Above the glowing strip it read, "3% Life remaining."

"Damn!" Jack exclaimed in frustration as hit his fist on the table.

He picked the computer up and scanned it all around, but found nothing.

Jack thought for a bit and looked at a clock, which read 5 A.M., as Laura came back downstairs.

"What happened? You're not watching anymore?" asked Laura.

"I think the battery ran out," replied Jack.

"Man..."

"Yeap..."

"So what are you going to do?"

"Take some days off and figure this thing out. You won't believe what I saw, I saw the inside of their entire ship, I mean this can't be just some movie, or someone playing a prank. I know this is for real, and I know it exists."

Laura slowly came next to him and put her hand on his shoulder. With her innocent eyes, which were filled with true love, gave Jack hope.

"Why did this thing only come to me? Why did it find me? I really didn't want this, God, I don't know..."

"It's not up to you, it's something you must do. You sent your vibration to the Universe to discover something of this sort, and it heard your call," said Laura.

Laura showed a bit of arrogance. She knew Jack's ability and mind and she didn't want to give-up on him. Laura had more confidence in him than Jack himself.

"Besides, I make twice as much as you, so I won't have a problem running this house till you get this sorted out. My condo is all paid off, and I don't have too many bills."

Jack and Laura were in silence for a while looking into each other's eyes. They were slowly realizing that they needed one another in this life, and not in just one situation. Jack felt blessed by God to have someone like her come into his life.

"You'll do that for me?" asked Jack.

"I wish you could've asked earlier, I would've done it a long time ago," replied Laura with love in her eyes.

Tears came out of Jack's eyes as he stood helplessly in front of Laura. "I am so sorry I didn't see the real you earlier."

"All I can say is that you better stick to your promise of the 4th day."

Jack put both his hands on her face and smiled with happiness.

"Here," he reached into his pocket and took out his keychain, and took the house key out from the ring.

"Today this belongs to you."

Laura smiled cleverly. "What?" Jack asked, as he suspected something by her look.

Laura reached into her pocket and took out a bunch of keys. She made duplicates of all the keys from Jack's keychain.

"Sorry, I already made arrangements."

"Oh, you little devil."

"Sorry," replied Laura.

Laura faced the machine while in his arms. She felt such comfort that hadn't been experienced in a long time.

Laura's eyes squinted as she observes something. The life meter on the KYIRUX computer started to slowly increase. Scanning the computer she saw a thin ray of sunlight starting to appear from the basement window.

"Jack," Laura whispers.

"Yeah," replied Jack.

"I think I know what makes the computer work."

"What?"

"Solar power perhaps..."

Jack took Laura out of his arms and glanced at KYIRUX. He, too, noticed the increase in the computer energy as the ray of sunlight shined on the logo; he went over to the device and scanned it with his curious eyes, he then took the table and placed it directly under the rising Sun. The energy drastically increased.

Jack quickly placed his hands over the glowing keyboard. And again a red button appeared.

Jack pressed the button and came back to the world of Pascal.

Surrounded by the white light Jack curiously waited for Pascal to appear. Laura smiled at his boyish curiosity and joins him in his new mission.

SYIRUX-82 logo was glowing on the backside of the ship. Pascal came and sat on a rock outside and looked directly into the screen, feeling extremely devastated.

He looked worried with stress in his eyes. The excitement from his face had vanished, as he started the video journal:

"Time is 24:44. We have a total of 120 crew members on this ship at the time, with 9 tons of animal weight and 55 TARI tons of engineering on this craft. I have just learned that we may have to dispose some things, but I will not do so on your planet, I have a place for them."

"The presence of heavy moon gravity and a mysterious gas in the atmosphere is weakening the magnetic molecules in the laser jet engine. This is something we haven't encountered before on our mission. At this rate we cannot stay here more than 700 minutes."

Pascal took a brief pause and kept looking into the video pen.

"To whomever it may concern or whoever may find this video journal in the eternity of time and space, I will tell you a little about us and who we are, and why we are here."

A thick transparent monitor appeared behind Pascal through a small device. The screen showed the interior body of these aliens' beings.

The body of these creatures consisted of 94% that of humans. It had the same skull, rib cage, pelvis, leg and hands. Pascal then did additional work on the graph board, as organs begin to appear. The bodies of these aliens had 2 beating hearts, with 2 kidneys, 2 livers and a stomach divided into two parts. What seemed to be an animated presentation; showed bone structure of the creatures, as muscle covered the entire skeleton, with the skin in a synced animation.

"This is our interior and exterior body, the two hearts and two livers with a pair of kidneys, lungs and stomach. Our eyes have seven layers of lenses, which helps us zoom in & out on any object of up to 3 miles. The average age of our species runs about two to three hundred years, considering an entire rotation of our planet takes 588 days to make full circle around our star Aditya, as I am turning 168 in 47 hours."

He then showed the inside of the skull where the brain rested. "This is our brain, a computer like thinking organ. Every living and breathing species on this Universe has one; it's not an option for an intelligent life. It's a must. Throughout our time we have come to learn the fact, that for the first seventeen million years of our existence we only used 2.1% of our brain capacity. Then, our scholars discovered a new method of mind meditation that opened up many nerves in the brain, which were never used before.

The language that I speak of is called Eolith; it's a universal language among the aliens whose mouth is shaped like our own with exact same vocal cord. With this kind of mouth and vocal cord, one can speak up to 35 thousand languages. The figure I am giving you may not make any sense to you and your world. In our life time we have not encountered any other form of intelligent life, only marine life under the icy moons of various planets including planets themselves. It could be a coincidence or it could be the nature of Universe. But, this planet and the fourth from this star have strong potential for creating intelligent life. This is why we have landed here, to find out the reason for such a miracle, although there may be one more possibility of life on this celestial system, because, I feel its power, I feel it has some control over me, and I need time to figure it out."

"Today I know I have changed your life, I only wish that you can change ours. I don't know whether we'll get to the White Gates, but the reason why we're going there is because of an invitation. Yes.... an invitation, we received it in form of a mathematical laser signal from trillions of light years away. The signal is so old, I do not know if their world still exists, but our curiosity has led us 757 light years away from our own planet. I know 757 light years is nothing, but we're trying to find the Event Horizon that exists in this solar system. Event Horizon is a space no larger than an eight hundred yard crater, which bends space and time, to reach from one place to another within a matter of seconds. There are millions of Event Horizons all over this Universe. The one that will get us closest to White Gates exists in this Solar System; we just have to find it."

At this time the button started to glow back & forth, as Jack and Laura observed it carefully.

"How do we continue?" said Jack.

Suddenly Pascal came back on the screen.

"If you understand what I am saying press the blue button."

Jack glanced over and saw the blue button glowing.

He pressed and Pascal continued with his historical journey.

Jack rubbed his eyes, as they looked heavy from not getting any sleep for the past 24 hours.

"Through our calculation, if life is generated on this body of rock it will be considered intelligent in approximately 425 million years from now. Although we do not know how you will evolve and how your body and shape will develop, I hope it is good enough to look for us and help us find those who gave birth to us. And if we do reach there before you, then we'll openly welcome you. I say this because; in the 4th demission, our bodies, mind, and soul do not die off, they stay the same, for as long as this Universe is breathing."

Pascal stared at the camera, wanting to say something.

"I will take you on a journey and show you something that you may have never seen before, and that is our home, our world and our base of knowledge, planet Divya-82."

"But before you come with me on this journey, I have to make you aware of a few things. By the time my message reaches you; this body of planet would've slowed down in its rotation by 8 hours and its satellite would push back 1.2435556 inches per 363 days. It will take you around 6 hours to complete this tour, where you'll find everything about us and our world, and perhaps I hope it provides knowledge for your world to advance its technology."

"On this tour you won't need any protection, you'll be submerged into hygroglaphic gel, inside a tube, that will make you feel, touch, smell and sense the beauty of our planet at the time we left, and how it might look now."

Pascal showed an animation of an eye. "A naked eye of our species is able to see more than 9 colors."

When talking about the different colors, he presented a pallet of each individual color on his screen.

"Red, Green, Blue, Yellow, Black, White, Ultra Violet and Infra Red- These are the basic colors that 79.7% of this Universe is made of. Yet there was one color that our eyes had never seen. We couldn't have imagined this color could exist, but only our eyes are strong enough to see this color and its light. The animals in our world didn't have strong enough sight to view it, and went blind. We did capture some rocks that were of this color, which rest in our laboratories. I would show it to you, but you may go blind."

"This particular planet, which carries this color, lies about 3.3 light years away from this star system; and we will show you, how to build an object at such speed, that will help you explore that body and the Universe itself."

Jack and Laura sat still, agonizingly awaiting Pascal's next instruction.

"At this time if you press the two glowing buttons together, it will start the process of your journey. Just step on the glowing plates, let KYIRUX do the rest, and I shall see you after."

The screen defused, while the bright sunlight hit Jack and Laura's face.

"I think I am going to have a heart attack, what about you?" Jack asked Laura.

Looking straight at the computer she replied, "I think I might have had one already."

"Oh God, why this, why now, I can't think..." Jack is now in a very paranoid mood. He looked into Laura's eyes.

"What do we do now?" Jack asked.

"Well! So you want to pack up the luggage or should I?" replied Laura.

Jack glanced at his watch.

The time read "6:00 AM."

"I got to wake up the kids soon. Then call-off work for the day and figure everything out."

"You mean quit."

"Now wait, we're going to think about all this first, may be a few days can solve this thing, it might be a hoax by some kid," replied jack.

"Jack, this has changed your life and career forever, you can't go back, I won't let you, and this is no joke, no kid can make a device this advanced."

Jack grinded his teeth and seriously thought about everything.

"I am not calling NSC."

"Good," Laura replied, "but who will you call?" she asked.

Jack looked at a certain point in the room and smiled.

CHAPTER 5

STRUGGLING TO THINK

Jack and Laura were preparing breakfast for themselves and the kids. The smoke winds away from the frying pan as sizzling bacon and eggs were being prepared. On the other pan held 2 small T-Bone steaks. Laura sat on the other side beating eggs. Her beautiful curls came in front of her eyes as she fixed them with her hand while holding a wooden spatula. She reminded Jack of a very dedicated wife and a mother that only existed in his dreams, but never more.

"Steak, are the kids going to eat this?" Laura asked in a concerned manner.

"No… this is just for me," Jack replied.

"What about me?" Laura questioned.

"I…can make you some," replied Jack.

"Will you please!" she replied with an attitude.

Jack nodded his head and went into the fridge and pulled out another piece of steak. He put all the chili powder and other spices and seasoning on the meat, and within twenty seconds threw it on the pan.

"Are you going to tell anyone else about this?" Laura asked while pouring eggs in the pan.

"I don't know. I don't even know if I should tell the kids."

"If you do tell the kids, they will be excited to tell everyone in their class and their friends."

"I know, I just don't know I have to figure all this out after dropping them off."

Lisa came into the kitchen, went straight up to Laura and wrapped herself around her legs with a smile.

"Hey you come here," Laura picked Lisa up in her arms.

Jack watched the happiness on his daughter's face and just observed.

"How was your sleep?" asked Laura.

"I had a dream in the morning I think," Lisa replied.

"In the morning uh, you know what they said about dreams in the morning?" said Laura as she walked with Lisa in her arms to pick up a loaf of bread.

"What do they say?" replied Lisa.

"They say… if you have a dream of something in the morning it becomes true."

"Really?" asked Lisa.

"Yes, so what did you dream about?" Laura asked Lisa while making the omelet.

"I dreamed that you were my mom, and we were shopping for Michael and dad's cloths in the mall during Christmas time."

Jack and Laura looked at each other as Jack was speechless; and suddenly emotions could be felt between the two.

"Well, maybe one day it will come true," said Laura.

Michael came running into the kitchen and went straight to Laura.

"Laura, you are still here," said Michael as he wrapped himself around her leg.

"Hello… I am in the kitchen as well, you know," said Jack while he waved at the kids.

Both the kids just smiled, as they glanced at him while Lisa winked her eye at Jack.

Jack glanced outside the window and pondered about his life in the last 24 hours. His eyes and face revealed a confused state of mind. He wanted to put his hand in his arms and close his eyes. He even tried to do that on the ledge of the window, but suddenly the door bell rang. He quickly walked to the door. Laura stood up, glanced at Jack in suspicion. Looking into the peep hole he saw Steve Herman, his neighbor standing at the door.

"Steven… what are you doing up so early, everything ok with you and your wife," Jack asked.

"Hey does the cow have a bell?" replied Steve.

Jack laughed and invited him inside the house.

"Come on in," said Jack, trying his best to act normal.

"Nah … I am just on my way to work, but just wanted to know if everything was ok last night?"

"What do you mean ok?"

"Well I was hearing all kinds of noises and seeing lights coming from your basement window, so I thought I would check."

Jack didn't know what to tell him. He knew he can't tell the truth, but needed a quick cover-up. Jack opened the door so Steve could see Laura sitting and eating breakfast.

"Ah, all I can ask now is… how was it?" Steven asked.

Jack without using his vocal cord only moved his mouth.

"Adventurous," he said in excitement.

"Very nice, well, I gotta get on the road. I'm getting late tiger, be safe."

"I will partner," Jack replied and closed the door as Steve walked down the steps.

"Who was it?" asked Laura.

"Steve from next door, asking about all the fireworks in the basement last night," replied Jack.

Laura got up and came closer to Jack.

"What did he ask? And what did you tell him?"

Jack hesitated a bit.

"What?" She again questions him.

"He was asking about the noise and the lights coming from the basement last night."

"Ah ha, and what did you tell him?" asked Laura.

"I ah… ah, I just kind of told him that, um."

At this time Laura became curious.

"What did you say?"

"I just showed him you and the kids eating breakfast."

Jack quickly moved into the kitchen, went over to the sink and started washing the dishes.

"I don't believe this, you actually told him we..."

"Sh... the kids," said Jack, putting his hand on Laura's lips.

Laura quickly lowered her tone looking at the kids, and then she came right next to Jack.

"Great, so now I am just an excuse to the world," replied Laura in a nagging manner.

"Ok, it's time for their school, I think you better get moving," said Laura.

"Ok look I am sorry I just had to cover this whole thing up, now please can we talk about this afterwards," replied Jack, in an apologetic tone.

"You bet we're going to..." replied Laura.

Quickly changing her tone and mood Laura went back into the dining room, where the kids were almost done eating their breakfast.

Snow fell over the town of Pennsylvania during a beautiful sunrise. Jack's house was covered with a pure white sheet of ice. Coming out of the house, Jack lifted Lisa up into his arms. She looked precious wearing a red beanie with a white sweater. Holding her small little water bottle and a backpack; Lisa put her hands out into the falling snow while wearing red gloves. Laura carried Michael on her waist and twirled, as she pointed to the falling snow.

"What the hell? I didn't hear anything about any snow the last couple of days," said Jack while scanning the sky.

"You must have been really busy with something," said Laura.

"Yeah, but it's weird though, Sun is still shining, and snow is falling, strange, isn't it?" said Jack.

On the street, right in front of the porch, was a Yellow school bus. He and Laura took the kids and put them on the bus as Jack kissed Lisa, and Laura kissed Michael on the cheek.

"Bye buddy, I'll see you in the evening," said Laura to Michael as she waved at the kids.

"Oh, wait." Laura reached into her jacket pocket and took out two bars of chocolate. She handed one to Michael and the other to Lisa.

"Is this white chocolate?" Michael asked.

"Always, I know what my boy likes," replied Laura.

"Do you know I've already had eight visits to the dentist in the past year?" Jack told Laura.

"It's sugarless, they won't even notice," replied Laura.

The kids waved back, as they got seated in the bus which started to slowly roll away.

Jack then amusingly glanced towards Laura and after a few moments became serious.

"Can I trust you?" asked Jack.

"Just speak to me," Laura replied while frustrated by Jack's 21 questions every hour. She still couldn't believe he was still questioning her trust.

"I don't want to prolong this issue for another tenth of a second. I see your eyes, I know who you are, and I trust you."

"You better trust me," replied Laura as she walked back towards the house.

"Wait," Jack yelled.

"What?" replied Laura as she turned around.

"Come with me," said Jack.

"Where?"

"To finally see him," replied Jack.

"You mean after all these years you're finally going to see…"

Jack nodded his head.

"Yes, the big guy…" Jack replied as he walked inside the house.

While entering the door he quickly took the shovel and started cleaning the porch filled with snow. Laura enjoyed the view and the weather. She also paid attention to the sexy man who was clearing the snow with his previously underestimated muscles. Looking around on the ground she kneeled and picked up a good amount of snow in her hand. She rolled it with both hands and made a ball out of it.

"Hey Ph.D. boy," called Laura while Jack wasn't paying any attention to her but did care to reply.

"Yeah," he answered while busy in his work.

"Can you calculate the time of a half pound object being thrown from fifteen feet away?"

Jack still didn't look at her but gave her an answer. "I don't know depends on how fast the object is traveling. Why?"

After replying he quickly glances at Laura who was fixing the snowball in her hand.

"Oh hell no….don't you even dare…." said Jack as he panicked and put the shovel down on the side. After a few seconds he slowly began to step back towards the door.

Laura didn't say a word nor did she make any expression on her face and faked throwing the snowball. Jack ducked for cover, but once he did, she quickly threw a fastball and hit his head. The hard cold ice left a freezing imprint on his bright red face. Jack too grabbed a pile of snow and threw it at Laura; who screamed and threw more snow back.

Jack ran up to her, grabbed her as they both fell on the bed of ice. Laura kept throwing snow at him, as he held her hand and laughed out loud. While looking at her, he did show some concern on his face.

"Thank you, I feel my heart beating again," said Jack.

Laura simply stared at him and gave him a quick kiss.

It was a moment that should've been framed in the stillness of time.

Jack and Laura rushed downstairs, as sunlight diminished from atop of KYIRUX. But in the small amount of time that the Sun had shined, it gave a sufficient amount of power to the computer.

Quickly, Jack grabbed the whole dolly and moved it over to a corner of the basement. He took-off the sheet from the wall and opened his secret locker combination.

Slowly Jack opened the door but then stopped and glanced over to Laura.

"Just open the damn door," said Laura.

Jack smiled and opened the door to the secret safe.

The door opened and showed scientific gadgets but of an unusual kind. He then took the computer and put it in the safe and locked it.

"Let's go," said Jack.

CHAPTER 6

MEET Mr. JOHN

University of Pennsylvania, Mathematics Building

A cloudy day at the University where more than the usual crowd was present and a small club fair was in progress.

Inside the hall the voice of someone lecturing could be heard, but it was low and faded. The voice gradually became clearer by the seconds as Jack and Laura came up to a classroom hall. Upon arrival at the door, a huge lecture room was being used by at least 90 students.

Jack fixed his hair and his shirt as he peaked inside the lecture hall. Wearing a half sleeve shirt and a tie with his belly hanging out, 75-year-old professor John Crawford, who had been teaching at the University for 25 years with great affability (and a bit of a character on the side), was in the middle of telling a story.

"So in 1965 when misses and I were done with our tango and we headed back to the cabin; now I don't mean to brag but I was one hell of a shaker," said John Crawford as he shakes his waist in front of the class while everyone started laughing.

"I am sure all of you wonder; what was the one crazy thing to come out of that whole night?" said John, as he diverted his attention towards the left side where Jack and

Laura were standing. He carefully looks at the door and realized who it was.

"Ladies and gentlemen," said John as he walked over to the door, held Jack's hand and dragged him inside the classroom.

"This man is the crazy thing to come out of that night, my son Jack."

An embarrassed Jack began frantically shifted his eyes as all 90 students laughed their hearts out.

"Dad what the hell are you doing? This is why I don't call you anymore," whispered Jack in anger.

"He's a bit shy as you can all see," said John.

Jack gave a fake smile at the crowd, then dragged John out while Laura was laughing hysterically.

"Oh my, and who is this beautiful thing, is she your girlfriend Jack?"

"Dad, please," replied Jack.

"So she's not, well I know a woman this beautiful can't be psycho enough to be with this Jackass.

"What's your name honey?"

"Laura," she replied.

"Really, my wife's name was Laura," said John pleasantly.

"Really?" asked Laura as she glanced at Jack.

"Oh yes," replied John.

"Ok, can we do this social introduction some other time," said Jack.

"Stop holding my arm," said John as Jack was trying to drag him away from the classroom.

"Sorry dad, but you need to come with us right now."

"Wait, the class isn't over for the next ten minutes."

"Yeah, I see what you're teaching in there."

"Hey, now that's good stuff," said Laura.

"Will you stop encouraging my dad?" said Jack.

"OYE! Don't yell at her, I'll have to kick your ass," John told Jack angrily.

"Ok dad! I need some time with you and it's very urgent."

"What, you blew up the barbeque again. Jesus. How long as it been, two thousand?"

"You mean it happened more than once," Laura asked John.

"Oh wait till I get started on him, we're not just talking about barbeque we're talking about rockets."

"Dad!"

"Alright, alright, stay here and don't touch anything in the hallway," said John, as he walked back inside the class.

"Ok people, I have to go fix my son's barbeque again, yes I know today was very important but we'll finish up how Jack acted during his puberty days on Monday."

"I really love you dad!" Jack cried to John sarcastically.

Jack, Laura and John came and sat down inside the university café.

"Alright what the hell is on your mind?" asked John.

"Ok, you remember the string-theory and molecule separation you talked about in 1993, about how a human body can be transferred from one place to the other in an instant," said Jack.

"Yea," John replied.

There was a long pause by Jack, as silence extended amongst the three of them.

"I think I might need your help on that subject," said Jack.

"What? You created a new monster now, what has he been up to?" said John as he glanced at Laura.

"Um..."

"Dad, I know how we might have gotten here."

"Really; because I saw you coming in a spaceship you parked in the second floor," John replied and laughed by himself.

"I am talking about us human's dad, I need to know, if I were to try something like that, what will happen to me?" asked Jack.

"You mean, you actually made something like that?" John replied as he glanced at Jack.

"No! I might have found something like that," replied Jack.

"Where?" asked John.

"Come with me," replied Jack.

This whole time Laura was just sitting next to Jack watching them talk without interruption. It interested her to see two brilliant men, one senior and one junior, talk about something as if they were innocent little children again.

The door to Jack's locker opened as he pulled out the computer and laid it on the tool-cart again. John watched in curiosity trying to figure out this thing his son just pulled out.

"What the hell, what is this?" John asked.

Jack didn't reply for awhile. His father looked at him straight in the eye and asked again.

"What, answer me?"

"How is your cholesterol?" Jack questioned his father.

"What?"

"Your Cholesterol?"

"Not good," John replied.

"I think you might want to sit down for this dad."

John got suspicious.

"You got a chair," asked John.

"Oh yeah," replied Jack.

John sat on the chair across Jack while Laura sat on the stairs. Jack told him everything, what had happened to him in the laps of time. He showed him the buttons, the lights, and the early messages of Pascal.

By the end of it John had tears in his eyes and, was speechless, without any answers for Jack.

"What should we do dad?" asked Jack.

"This, this has… if I die today I know I will be able to deal with eternity with some sort of satisfaction," replied John.

"I know you've never listened to me before but I will tell you, don't go to the big boys, this thing will be extinguished before you can even blink your eyes, and no one in the world will ever hear about it again," said John.

"Well the next step is to go through the journey then," said Jack.

"Yeah, that's right, we'll have to," John replied.

"So you think it's safe?" asked Jack.

"First let's see your travel kit, press the button," said John.

Jack pressed the button that was supposed to show their traveling device. The computer suddenly started to change shape. The bottom two rods began to grow and suddenly they moved onto the ground, where the computer now had legs and stood up without support.

Down at the bottom, two huge plates appeared with a 66-inch radius, glowing blue lights around the border.

Jack and John stepped back as the computer started to morph itself into a gigantic shape. The glowing border from the plates started to grow and became a glass cylinder.

John watched like a little kid, as Pascal was an eternal answer of spirituality for him. His face lit up again seeing this computer manifest itself like a science fiction book. Once the device had finished changing shape, Pascal began preparing them for their journey.

"This is the beginning construct of the journey. The three-lit plates you see is the launching pad, its original program was to convert your cells into electronic magnetic field and transfer you into the distant place with the same console. But by the time you find the computer, our world might already be destroyed by a natural or unnatural cause. This is why you'll be getting only the virtual tour, which is much safer and without any biological risks."

"It's a 2% possibility for Divya-82 to be functioning as a living breathing planet. This journey will not take your physical bodies to our planet; just your mind. Through this device you'll be peaking at our home from the bended space. KYIRUX will be able to bend space to an extent where only your mind will see a live picture of our solar system and Divya-82, in current time.

"Our world might look like the kingdom of God, but don't mistake our superior intelligence for arrogance. We have made big mistakes, big enough to end the life of our own planet at one point.

"Divya-82 produced a black material EXIAN PATROL; it's a material that helped us provide power in vehicles, houses, electricity, fire and many more useful things that required consumption of this material. Luckily, we were able to find out the disadvantage of this lucrative material before it was too late. This oil was actually a necessity for our planet to spin and rotate around Aditya. If we would've consumed it for 50 more years; Divya-82 would've stopped spinning on its axis, which could have led to a major shift in the weather and ozone layer. This is why I hope that this tour will give you more education on creating useful resources instead of consuming or destroying your planet itself, because besides the living beings on a planet, the planets themselves need to survive off their resources."

The computer shut-off and the button started to glow. Jack started to press the button.

"Wait!" said John.

"Don't you want to come?" said Jack.

"I need to sit down. This explains the whole global warming here on Earth. The more oil they pump, the higher their stock goes, and higher our chances of being instinct increases. I guess this must be the economic soul of this Universe. Consume and move on," said John.

"Makes you wonder doesn't it, Laura you're ready?" asked Jack.

"Wait, you think I am coming with you?" Laura told Jack.

"Yeah...," Jack replied.

"Well here is a little thought before you take your vacation, actually one word, children."

"This thing will be over in less than six hours, it's just a tour," said Jack.

"I know that," Laura replied.

"Don't you want to see what the alien world looks like, and the way they live or might have lived?" said Jack.

"I do, but, I need to be here in case something goes wrong," replied Laura.

"Wait both of you, it's only bending the space, which is possible according to some scientists, but the only thing that worries me is…falling out of that bend of space and time."

"What do you mean?" Laura asked.

"When you're traveling as the space bends itself, it's a very narrow area that you're body is squeezed into, three to four feet can throw you off to a land where hell will seem more comfortable," replied John.

"These people are millions of times more advanced than us, their mistakes don't occur 1 out of ten times. It's more like 1 out of million times," Jack explained.

"I guess those loose monkey looking creatures explain a lot about their rare mistakes…Jack. They are us and we are them, mistakes happen with or without our consent. Nobody's perfect, that's the first rule, before you search for intelligent life. Intelligent life is only created upon mistakes."

"I thought we wouldn't be able to contact alien life for the next 10 thousand years, didn't even realize it was here millions of years before us," said John.

Jack took a seat knowing the truth that lay before him. He thought for a while but couldn't come up with any quick solutions.

"All my life you told me to believe in the unreachable, not to hold myself back by rules, not to ever let go of a moment that can define the faith of men or oneself. Those things stuck by me and I left NSC due to those beliefs, but this is that one moment dad, and it's not just me, but you as well have a chance to be a part of it."

"All that changed when your mother passed away. This philosophical nonsense holds no meaning when you let go of your best friend in your arms; only the things you attach your emotions with hold all the meanings for a person, and you're number one on that list."

Jack glanced over to him with love.

"Well, if we did blow up, at least it'll be together," said Jack.

"Ok why are we spreading such negativity here? This is just a fieldtrip remember, no one is going anywhere from here," said Laura.

"You still got something in that bottle I gave you on your birthday, or anything else for that matter?" John asked.

"I still do, enough for all three of us," Jack replied.

"Bring it on, but you do really suck for still not finishing that thing up," said John.

"You can't drink and drive you know," said Jack while grabbing the bottle from the shelf and three shot glasses from a nearby cabinet.

Jack poured a shot in each of the three shot glasses. He then handed one to his father, and one to Laura.

Jack raised the glass in front of his father for a toast. But before he could say anything John took down the whole shot. Jack didn't have anything to say as he stared at his father.

"What?" questioned John innocently.

"Nothing dad…" replied Jack as he took back his shot.

Laura took her shot down as well. Jack glanced back at the computer sitting in the basement as his mind relaxed.

He glanced at it with extreme emotions but lowered inhibitions. The two plates in the bottom were glowing and waiting for someone to step on them.

John noticed the exposed corner of the chalkboard. He squinted his eyes and fixed his glasses. He got up and walked to the board and slowly took the sheet off the last part of the board. He read the mathematical equation very carefully.

"When the hell did you do this?" said John.

Jack turned around and aimed his eyes at the board.

"I was bored," replied Jack.

John stared at the sheet and openly looked at the whole mathematical equation.

He started from the beginning of the equation and slowly worked his way to the end.

Laura glanced at Jack in a questionable manner.

His father suddenly halted towards the end of the board. He lifted his glasses up and started thinking.

Jack then noticed his father in complete concentration.

"What? What is it?" Jack asked.

"You actually made some sense, for the first time in your life," replied John.

"Really, thank you for finally noticing it," replied Jack.

"You really think this planet will be passing by that soon?" asked John.

"I am only human, I could be wrong," replied Jack, while John moved his eyes at the computer.

"So what do we do now?" Laura asked both of them.

"Well! Its only six hours, I guess we buckle up," Jack replied.

Jack went to the computer and stood an inch away from the glowing plate. He was scared to step on it. He knew what would happen if something was to go wrong. John on the other hand came and stood on his plate immediately.

Suddenly the plate became red and stated, "overweight" as a third plate came along and went right underneath the first plate. It then came back to glowing green.

"Well… I have put on a few pounds," said John while he held this stomach and sucked it in.

Jack and Laura were amused by his presence.

Jack came and stood on the plate as well. Laura got a little worried.

"So it's only you two," Laura asked.

"Kids, remember," Jack replied.

"Plus if his ass blows out of the sky then at least you can claim this slum hole in your will," said John.

"Ok! What is that suppose to mean Mr. John? I am sorry but I need to go with Jack," Laura said while in panic.

"But this is only for overweight," replied John.

"Laura, I need someone here for the kids, and I need someone they can trust."

"Okay…," replied Laura, knowing the delicacy of the situation.

"I will come back, okay; ready to do this dad?"

"You bet your ass I am, sorry missy."

John got off from his plate and hugged Jack and started kissing him on the cheek and forehead. Jack got irritated and shrugged him off his face. John also hugged and kissed Laura on the forehead.

When he walked back, while passing Jack he kissed him on the cheek again.

"Alright, dad, dad, leave the slobbering for the dog."

"I love you," John told Jack.

"Ok, you're creeping me out," Jack replied.

Jack quickly changed his tone and attitude and proceeded to walk onto the disk, but then came back and kissed Laura.

"Okay, okay enough, let's get moving," said John.

"Quit slobbering and go…" Laura replied.

"Yes madam," Jack replied.

Jack went back on the plate and pressed the red button. Suddenly the interior of the plate began spinning and a blue light surrounded Jack & John. A liquid type substance started filling the cylinder as it glowed brightly. They both struggled to breathe, but then realized that they were curiously able to respire normally while submerged inside this glowing liquid.

Laura first watched in horror, then started to calm down after Jack smiled at her and gave her the thumbs up.

The thin blue light suddenly became thick and heavy enough to only show a blurred figure of Jack inside the cube.

John got hidden in the thick fog inside the cube as well.

Going through a multi colored maze of laser and lights, Jack's face began to stretch as the force was unbearable.

"God, I can use some chicken right now…" said John while getting his face and body stretched.

CHAPTER 7

CITY OF DOTAGE

Laura stood behind two cylinders while there was complete silence in the basement, as John and Jack were frozen in a thick green liquid.

They experienced darkness while inside the matrix of this vortex. Then, a very thin light appeared that gradually grew and led them right in front of a dark rocky wall. Jack carefully waited to reach the edge.

Arriving at the edge, Jack's panicked face suddenly turned into a smile. A shiny moonlight hit his face and with very thin air blew his hair. All he could do at that moment was be confused with happiness.

The land of frozen darkness stood still. It was an endless field of Ice, which had found a nest on every single thing that was in its way. The star (Aditya) still had some life left, but the energy was not enough to light this world that was so similar to ours. The gas in Aditya had been burned and used. There was also a smaller star which was now a white dwarf, quickly spinning light on both ends of its pole. A small but half broken moon watched its mother dying a slow death. This planetary system had two sources of energy with one satellite.

There were very uniquely shaped structures growing from the ground, while frozen in time and space, with no one to appreciate its beauty.

Jack had tears coming out, while John, too, had a tear dripping down his cheek. From the side Pascal came walking in front of them on the icy ground.

"This is our planet Divya-82; I do not know what kind of a condition you're witnessing. By this time, there may not be anything but empty space."

Pascal had recorded this journal, perhaps billions of years ago, but even during his taping, he was emotionally curious to know about his planet. He asked Jack about the current conditions, and if sunrise and sunset was still as beautiful as it looked during his departure. But Jack had no words for him.

Jack suddenly got a white ray of light in front of him. He was frozen in time with his hand covering his eyes. The thick white fog started to clear up as Jack found himself inside a huge hall.

The structure had a sky dome that was throwing rays of Aditya light in a very unique shape. Jack removed his hands slowly and opened his eyes like a baby would for the first time.

After he observed the place, he witnessed human like aliens in mid-air, floating in a manner that made one assume that their palms controlled their flight. They were submerged in deep meditation, making the process seem harmless and painless. A few of these aliens were suspended ten feet in the air while meditating. In the very front of this group of people lay a huge piece of a crashed alien craft, rising from beneath the ground. It had become a symbol of deacon.

Jack crawled slowly amongst the people towards the white glowing ball, which sat next to this crashed spacecraft.

Inside the dome there was a deep base of "Om…" sound occurring. While Jack was crawling to the front in between people, Pascal came from the middle of the fog to appear in front of him.

"This is a sanctuary, something what you may say symbolizes superiority. The deep repeating *Om* sound that you're hearing is the Universal sound for peace. It is actually been proven by our scientists that Black holes have the same sound occurring inside them. It is proposed that this is what makes matter be at peace, once it is caught by its own gravitational force." Pascal came and sat right in front of Jack.

"This is no ordinary place, the land on which this spiritual structure was constructed ten million years ago, is the place we believe was the landsite of the aliens who gave birth to us. On this spot our ancestors found the skeleton of the spaceship and a message inside it, the message was encrypted in a mathematical language whose meaning we eventually decoded. We found out we weren't just created from evolution or natural causes, but that we are a plantation of our alien ancestors who once landed on our planet hundreds and millions of years ago. They also claimed to be from the third Universe. But nothing caught our attention more than the phrase third Universe. For so long we believed that the term Universe was a space that held everything together within its realm, but, we were wrong; there lies a greater entity than a single Universe."

"Universe is actually just a huge sphere of space which holds septillions of Galaxies and planets, but going beyond those thick walls of gasses you come upon not trillions, not billions, millions or even thousands, there are actually just 3 spheres of these Universes standing still in their own mystical space. What exists beyond them is something only the one who has seen it can explain it. Those are the ones we are in search for. They are the ultimate beings. Perhaps they are the ones who sent us the signal to White Gates, which exists 1.3 trillion light years away from these three spheres."

They might be the 4th level of the human species, which do not care for in this Universe, because they have created their own Universe. We are currently considered level II humans, who can control weather and element conditions on our planet, and we only rely on the solar energy to light up our world. But, we are well on our way to becoming the 3rd level humans, who are the gypsies of this Universe."

On the side was John, sitting with his legs crossed and listening to Pascal like a kid, while Jack had his own Pascal as they both were getting two separate tours, without knowing each other's presence.

"We as the citizens of this planet have only come to believe in one power above us. This Universe; it gives us birth and it destroys us. It knows when everything will end, and how it will end. However, some humans grew weary of this Idea and decided to create certain figures for us to follow. It worked for about two and a half thousand years. But, after that, our brain evolved and couldn't consider these facts as the moral stamp of our race. But that was our doom. Being ignorant to the ancient knowledge, we lost the most important thing that made us Divyans, our culture. But after a few bumpy generations, we came back to our spiritual roots."

Inside the dome, where some people performed heavy breathing exercises, they sat in the meditative position, exhaling and inhaling very quickly.

"These kinds of breathing exercises that our citizens are doing, completely heal the body without any use of medication. The doctors in our world stopped prescribing medication once a very spiritual man started preaching the ways of self-healing by simple deep breathing. That's all we needed to stay healthy, a good amount of pure oxygen. This phenomenon occurred after our governments began testing nuclear missiles on barren lands. They thought testing such missiles will be harmless, but they didn't realize the invisible fumes from those tests was destroying people's immune systems, and causing the most dangerous cancer known to our species; skin cancer. Once our world was on the verge of extension, the universe sent us this spiritual man, who knew the best way to cure a soul; to just enjoy what was given to us for free—Oxygen."

Pascal came close to Jack's face, "Now let me take you to where life found a new beginning."

A white flash occurred before Jack's eyes, as he was now inside a highly advanced hospital, where the nurses were robots who carried various items, played with kids and sat next to patients reading, talking and showing programs on the laser screen.

Inside, huge tanks filled with a special blue liquid where humanlike bodies were being repaired as family members watched from outside.

One of the alien's hands had been cut-off, which was being repaired with new tissues, muscle, vessels and skin from the advanced technology of these species.

Pascal came in front of one of the doors as he grabbed Jack's attention, "come inside with me," said Pascal.

"This is something new we have been working on, it'll be too old by the time you get this, but, we have just found a way to make a female pregnant using just a bright ray of light."

Inside the dark room were three doctors and two robots standing by a pregnant woman.

"This procedure is called Divine Light Path. We take the sperm of a male and put it inside a new and advanced chemical, which makes the unhealthy sperm into a very strong candidate for giving life. In this procedure we can alter one's genes. If we want the offspring to be violent, strong and built for destruction it can easily be done, If we want the child to be peaceful, a teacher, or perhaps a great scientist, it can also be transformed into such a chemical mixture, but usually we don't play with that, we let nature put its own magic in the mix."

Jack suddenly realizes something, and spoke of just one word, "Jesus."

Jack went around the doctors and observed everything that was being done in the room. He came very close to the woman's stomach as the ray of light was being exposed onto her belly. He then glanced at the happy woman who sat in quietness watching the miracle of science and nature taking place.

Jack stood up and went to the machine that created the ray of light. A green glowing liquid, which was being turned into a light through a magnifying glass, beamed a light towards the woman's stomach.

Pascal walked near Jack, "let's see what might have become of this life in a distant future."

Instantly, Jack and John found themselves on a bright day on the streets of planet Divya-82. A young man headed towards a stall, but it was no ordinary stall, it was filled with the global currency like an ATM on Earth. An old woman approached the machine and put her thumb on the scanner. She then proceeded as a significant amount of credit came out. The credit that came out from the machine was enough to make this young man greedy.

He quickly grabbed the woman's currency and propelled himself into the air with oddly shaped sneakers. The woman didn't do anything but press a red button on the box and laugh. She knew this boy had made a ridiculously dumb mistake by taking her money.

Within 5 seconds of pressing the button the police came rushing in an advanced hovercraft.

Pascal and Jack watched them go past with jet-speed towards the young man.

"This is how the young man would be caught and brought to justice in front of the highest degree of people, the nine judges. Where there are humans, there will be everything and anything you can imagine."

The young man in the air streamed off in his shoes but the police caught him by throwing a huge amount of blue liquid on his body that froze him in midair.

From underneath the vehicle, police fired a transparent box which grabbed the man and took him back to the authority's machine.

On the other side of the town, Pascal and John rose up high in the air viewing the entire city.

Structure number 1 lit on the right hand side.

"This structure is our capital building. This is where all of our world matters are discussed. Where from a single child to a two hundred year old person can walk in and will get the same respect and attention as the other."

Then structure 2 glowed, which was totally hidden inside the icy plate, but manifested itself into what it used to be when the Planet was alive.

"This is known as the Universal Center, this is where our world's best businessmen come and do trading of goods and currencies."

Around two thousand people were screaming and yelling while moving around in hovercrafts buying and selling stocks but in a much-advanced environment.

"And finally our main structure, the most important thing to me, my place of work, KYIRUX headquarters," said Pascal as the building frozen in time came back to life.

"I will now show you what our world looked like, when we departed from here nearly five hundred million years ago."

Jack carefully watched.

The ice covered land morphed into a living, breathing city. Most of the buildings were made of chrome and steel. Some buildings were 10 times higher than the former world trade center of New York. There were small white and silver disks flying in the air. Amongst them were very small numbers of colored aircrafts with flashing lights, which were traffic police patrolling the airways.

"I shall now take you down to the ground and show you the civilized society of my world."

On the ground were the citizens of Divya-82 running to their daily lives the same way people do on Earth, just a lot more advanced. Their clothing was something no human eye on Earth had seen before. Even being a million times more technically advanced than us, they were very simple and easy going on material things.

Moving through the streets, which were similar to Earth, one noticed a unique steel type material which was displaying various shades of current on opposing sides. Vehicles on the road ran without tires, simply in thin air. These cars were beautiful, uniquely shaped in style and no-where-close to being similar to anything driven on Earth.

Jack, like a kid, gazed at every bit of information around him as he moved throughout the city in mid air.

John on the other hand was enjoying the view and the world. He even caught himself paying close attention to the beautiful alien women passing by him.

They moved into a very small black glass. Behind the glass was perhaps the Divya-82's biggest mall. It was built of pure white walls and uniquely shaped doors that dissolve into thin air when people entered.

Inside the individual shops were Divyans shopping and buying everyday things, but their way of doing transaction was very different.

They were not using cash, check or credit cards. The laser beam behind the counter was scanning their eyes. There was security moving on discs in the air, watching over the customers. Jack rolled around the side of the mall looking everywhere he could. On the side, near a shop, was

John quickly eating three individual ice creams and candy bars.

In the basement Laura stood right in front of the stairs. Jack and John inside the tube were still frozen, as the green gel only showed the shape of their body, but no other details were visible. The thick fluid inside blurred them considerably, while small bubbles popped up from the bottom of the cylinders.

Her face was numb, it seemed like she wanted to move but she couldn't, as if something was holding her tightly.

Jack was now staring out from a skyscraper at the whole city during the evening; which was an incredible sight for anyone to witness, from the huge colorful artistic shaped monuments to the plethora of tall buildings, which sparkled across the seashore.

Jack's plate suddenly moved closer to one of the very tall buildings with great speed. He then noticed his father John coming from the other side as well.

"Dad!!!" screamed Jack.

Jack and John ducked, as they got within 20 feet of colliding with one another.

Red walls were surrounded with thin sheeted televisions and 3D commercials on the wall of a hovercraft company. It seemed like the interior of a building. On the left was a very long hallway without any visible end. On the ground, John lay on top of Jack while they both lay unconscious.

Jack slowly gained consciousness and opened his eyes. He felt the pain of his heavy father's body on top of him, while he tried to move him away.

"Dad, hey dad," said Jack as he shook him.

John suddenly woke and put his glasses back on his eyes.

"What? What is it?" said John.

"Am I dead or alive, I think I am dead, I seem to be in hell."

"Oh move dad, we're not dead," replied Jack.

They both stood up and looked around the empty room. Behind them seemed to be a receptionist desk, and the KYIRUX computer that Jack found, but in a white color scheme.

Jack went behind the desk and looked at the computer; his senses made him touch and feel everything around him.

In the corner there was a small rectangular shaped box, which had lots of different types of food inside, almost like a snack machine. John's curiosity went towards the vending machine. He came up to it, scanned for what he was interested in and pressed the button next to the small frozen meal. The button lit as it took one of the items under a blue light and within two seconds it turned it into a hot meal, which came out at the bottom. John picked the red plate up and observed the food.

"What is that?" said Jack as he noticed the dish.

"Let me eat it and tell you," replied John while picking up this awkward shaped meal and took it into his mouth.

When the meal entered his mouth, John suddenly became illuminated and surprised by its taste. He knew his tongue had never had something of this sort. John loved the meal so much his head started to spin. He controlled himself and went over to Jack.

"Eat it, don't ask any questions, just take a bite," said John, as Jack took a small piece of this unusual food.

He suddenly got excited "Good uh..." said John. They both looked at each other and ran to the same wall and started pressing all the buttons they could.

John pressed two buttons at a time, as meals came out steaming and sizzling right in front of him.

"Can food really taste this good?" asked Jack while chewing. John didn't answer, but kept eating the unique dishes one-after-an-other.

"Yes, it can be if all the natural resources are mixed together, something your planet is missing," said Pascal, while on the KYIRUX computer screen.

Jack stopped eating his meal and paid closer attention to Pascal.

"The location you're standing at is the head plant of our airborne vehicles called SKYTALKERS. This is where I started as one of the engineers on the craft about sixty years ago. This whole structure is made of IYONIC ZIYCON material, which can withstand winds of up to 2700 miles per hour, fire, heat up to 500,000 thousand degrees and has the explosive capability of about 55 nuclear tons of TNT. This type of material is not found beneath our planet but is actually a mix of about 4 different types of metals we found on our moon and other planets in our solar system. This structure can be moved from location to location as they are only attached to a magnetic foundation beneath the ground and are airborne as you can see outside the window."

They both looked outside the window towards the downtown city of this planet and saw an airborne building being landed on an empty spot. There was smoke coming from beneath the buildings as blue and red lasers charged it.

"We can manufacture these buildings in less than six hours of your planet time. Every structure you see outside is based on the same system as this building. We haven't had any disasters by nature for about fifteen thousand years."

The window disappeared and became a wall again.

"What you are eating right now is known as, "Dungaree," it's a type of plant which requires blue soil which is not available on your planet but is on your 8th body of rock from the sun. This particular soil can produce about 500 more vegetables, which your species has not eaten or experienced this far. These meals are the reason why we live 5 times longer than before we made such discovery. The codes of its genes are available on the computer that you found. I am hoping you are now advanced enough to create its clone for your experiments.

"This computer you have in your possession can study the brain of a person that is about 300 yards within its radius. It will only show itself to individual species that are more curious than any else about finding the truth of this Universe, and in utmost honesty. I suppose you are the lucky winner or winners of this contest."

"I would like for you to see more of my world," said Pascal as the computer screen shutoff.

"Boy he has really made my day," said John as he spoke with his mouth full of food.

The sound of a train like vehicle faded in as Jack and John both turned around and looked towards the direction of the sound. There, they saw two white dollies ready for them to jump on.

John started filling his jacket pocket with the food when the dolly arrived next to him. They both got inside the dolly, as Jack started to look for the belt. The two carts began to move inside a dark room, which was about the size of 5 football fields and showed robotic engineers working on a huge spacecraft.

While on their tour, Jack and John witnessed the assembly of all the aircrafts and cars in the factory as each vehicle was being installed within seconds.

Their dolly moved forward into all the different stations that were making these crafts. Along the way they came upon a door, which itself was ten stories high.

The door opened as the dolly arrived in a new facility, there, the construction of the SYIRUX-82 ship was underway with robots and Divyans all working together.

Among those people were Pascal and Lava working on the side of this huge ship, which had only been coded with 35% diamond. As their dolly passed by the ship, Pascal walked over to both of them.

"This is the main eagle of our ship which is being assembled to be taken into the vast space of this Universe. It's our first attempt to do something so big. The furthest we have gone so far is the nebula gas ring which is 1.876 light years away. There, we found obstacles and problems that may arise with trying to go any further. There are invisible gasses in this Universe that are easily capable of melting 97% of all material. Which is why we are now putting the Coronal glass on the ship, it's a type of rock, which is deep beneath all the moons of any planet in this Universe. We also found out that radio signals never go beyond these invisible gasses which surround every solar system, for that reason we had to invent the laser signal that can reach from one end of the Universe to the other. If your planet is in search of an extra terrestrial life, which may be same or less of technologic savvy as you; their signal will not reach your planet due to the gasses, which surrounds your solar system. You will have to set up a responding station beyond those gasses; even the laser signal that has to be sent out from that area must be 100% accurate."

Pascal simply walked back to where he had been working. Jack and John's cart moved further down and came back into the darkness and quickly became airborne.

Their cars arrived from outside the darkness into the middle of the city they explored earlier. This time it was more of a residential area of this world. But they were not just normal looking houses; they were shaped in a dome form with uniquely designed balconies and windows. It was twilight time as the houses were self glowing without any external lights, but from within the material of the wall.

"Unbelievable," whispered Jack as he got out from his dolly.

No presence of John was nearby, as again they had been separated from one another. In the streets the children were playing a very unusual game with huge blocks of dice while in mid air twisting and twirling. The kids glided on a special hover board hanging around 10 feet in the air. Their clothes were very colorful but of a very different material as cartoons and other funny characters actively played on their outfits.

Jack walked around the kids, looking at what they were playing. He then moved to another group of kids who threw small jet rockets into the air as they flew up to catch them on special shoes.

A red house was right behind Jack, with all its light lit at the main door. When it opened up, a rope of laser came and wrapped around one of the kids and took the little guy inside.

"Ok time for my studies guys, see you tomorrow," said the little boy who was being dragged inside, almost as if he knew it was coming for him. When the young boy got inside the rope, suddenly other laser ropes came out from the houses, dragging each child inside to their homes as they all said good bye to each other.

Jack went up to one of the doors of the houses and stopped, looked around and peaked inside through a tinted window.

He put his hand on the scanner in front of the door. After a few moments the door of the house dissolved as Jack entered inside.

Inside it was close to being a modern American home but in more advanced and elegant form. The living room was set up with the most beautiful furniture and nicely lit walls. The house was dust free and very clean. From the hallway came a robotic female who moved in a very flexible motion. She walked up to Jack and stood in peace.

"Welcome to the world of my master's life," said the robot while Pascal also entered the house.

"Cynthia, my grandson's robotic companion and teacher," spoke Pascal as he stepped inside the house behind Jack.

"She has been with him since birth."

"She's been like a mother to him, after my daughter died in a hover accident a year after his birth. Cynthia's brain processing power is about 55 quarts hertz, its 66% of a human brain, with an execution of 33 trillion signals per seconds, while humans are 88 trillion. Cynthia can be designed to act like any person except a killer. Her components are not made or programmed to be that way, nor will our world towers ever pass that bill. Come inside and see."

From the hallway came Pascal's grandson as he jumped into his arms.

"What are you doing Chintomana?" said the little boy.

"I am recording this for our alien friends, remember?" Pascal replied.

"Oh that's right, can I talk to them as well?"

"Sure you can just look into the camera."

"Hi, Mr. Alien I love you," said the little boy.

"This is Maxton, my grandson.

"Ok time for our fun studies, but before that my little Maxton will have to finish his dinner," said Pascal as Cynthia took him into the kitchen.

"Can I have the Amlish and Giovane?" Maxton asked Cynthia.

"Sure you can, and I'll add Zimmer and Cherries on them too," replied Cynthia as she held him in midair without any support and twirled him with her magnetic power while walking inside the kitchen.

"She completely adores him, I have to treat her like a human because as her interior components are not made of metal but actual muscles and bone structure, and she feels pain just like us and has feelings. Her life expectancy is guaranteed for 350 years after which the insurance policy will extend it upon request," Pascal started going upstairs as Jack quietly listened and followed.

They both reached upstairs as a chant of mantra faded in from one of the rooms. There was no carpeting on the floor. Rather, it was a shiny marble type material.

"210 cynum please," Pascal said out loud.

"The floor will feel a little warmer to your feet now as you walk on it."

He walked right into the closed door as it dissolved into thin air. Inside a man was sitting in front of the white glowing ball. He was chanting the word *"Ara-Kara."*

"This word 'Ara-Kara,' is known as sound of desire. If chanted with complete dedication, it can bring you material things that you desire within. It's just as important as the word 'OM,'" said Pascal.

"This is my son-in-law Kenyan, who only desires one thing; my daughter.

"We couldn't have achieved the technological marvels we have today, without the support of meditation in our lives. It helps increase the concentration of the brain, which pills and medication can never achieve."

Pascal moved as the door dissolved back in. He and Jack walk into another room, which didn't have any technological gadgets but rather a plain simple space.

"This is my daughter's room, and that is her on the wall. She never wanted to be surrounded by electricity or any form of technology, she always wanted to be the one with nature, and now she is."

"That's Laura," said Jack, as Pascal's daughter's face features were close to Laura's.

Pascal looked a bit emotional and down and Jack could feel his pain. He loved and missed his daughter, and that was what his eyes spoke of at the moment.

Pascal slowly glanced at the photograph of his daughter for a while and went into deep thought.

"I haven't been in this room since she passed away," He stepped out of the room and started heading down stairs without saying a word. Jack followed him but Pascal sat on the last step of the stairs and held his forehead.

Jack sat right next to him and tried comforting him by putting his hand on Pascal's shoulder, but the hand passed right through him and it seemed to disturb the electronic circuit of the tour. But in few moments Pascal came back to its original shape.

"I am sorry, I really am," said Jack to Pascal, even though he knew no one could hear him.

"Love and emotions as you know, don't advance with time and technology; they stay as they are, in their natural form given by this Universe. Nothing can kill it and no-one can avoid its realm," said Pascal.

"I apologize for a sudden distraction; let me continue with the tour."

Jack walked into the kitchen but as he entered, Cynthia brought in a tissue and handed it to Pascal.

"I hope I am giving my best to be like Agithan," said Cynthia.

"You don't need to try, I love you as you are," replied Pascal as he gave her a kiss on her forehead. "I do not know where Maxton would be without you, I thank you."

Cynthia bowed, and smiled with respect.

"This could be considered a normal life on our planet, with lots of love and emotion on the side."

Pascal went into the kitchen and sat with his grandson and Cynthia, as he listened to Maxton talk about the new game he played at school that day.

"Nothing changes," said Jack as he watched them from a distance. Jack turned around and walked outside the door. The night had fallen as the streets were glowing from the houses and flying cars up above. From Jack's left side the very soft sound of a working machine faded-in. When he turned around Jack was shocked at what he saw. A robotic freeway bridge was coming together with its other half right above his head, almost as if it was becoming a bypass. The two freeways joined together as they came from each side.

After merging together for five seconds heavy traffic started flowing. The cars were very unique in shape and color. The ambience around jack was almost like an amusement park. He saw John in a vehicle speeding on the freeway. John held both of his hands in the air, like at a Disneyland ride.

"This is construct bypass. These types of bridge freeways have timing during the rush hours. When there is heavy traffic they emerge from the ground to create a six-lane bypass for the drivers. There has never been a rush hour jam on our planet for around five hundred years now. Even though 80% of our vehicles are airborne, some people still prefer the road," said Pascal, as he stood at the doorsteps to his house waving at Jack.

Sky scrapers ruled the planet of DIVYA-82; they were so tall that they actually came to the edges of the atmosphere. Inside each one was a very clean and neat environment, people were working, eating and walking in a very elegant and rich manner. The skyscrapers were only meant for the ones who could afford it. Economy and politics as it seemed, survived like a parasite on every corner of Universe.

Going down on the "real" ground and coming on land was a whole different story. Los Angeles is what can be compared to some of the streets of the town. It was raining heavily below as town citizens were carrying dome laser umbrellas, as comparatively advanced technology still existed even in "ghetto" areas where people were living below a poverty line.

City citizens were hanging on the corner of a certain place where only colorful light and the movement of shadows could be seen. Airborne cars stopped as young men and women got out and walked inside a club while small advance stalls were cooking food for the regular public. Like a hot dog stand on Earth, a man was giving away oddly shaped food. The customers scanned their hands on the monitor, instead of paying.

In the corner of the street, men standing outside looked highly intoxicated, yet not from drugs, pot or alcohol but from what they were listening to in their ears. A strange man walked up to one of the people and handed him a small black disk. In exchange the man gave him a glowing blue disk. He took the disk and put it in a small device that led up to his electronic ear-plugs and the man suddenly began to feel high and hallucinated.

Moving inside a club house was a display of strange mix of lightning, but without music. The ambience was like an after party in a club.

There were couches and beds everywhere. People were laying on top of each other listening to the addictive music in their headphones. Behind the bar table, John was wearing the same headphones while lost in his own world. In his hand was a pink glowing tube, as he took a sip from it.

"Oh my God, heavy, this is heavy man..." said John while laughing quietly.

Pascal was sitting right next to John, who was completely high, and smiling with his eyes closed.

"You feel stress free don't you?" asked Pascal as John nodded his head.

"It is mind stimulating music. The sound influences your neural bypass synoptic gaps, which your technology won't be able to point for another twenty years. Everything is timed in this Universe, you can't force yourself to be more or less advanced, it all comes into place by itself, and perhaps this is why you and I met, when time allowed it."

Pascal relaxed his head on the wall, sitting next to John; while John finishes up his drink.

"Oh yeah baby," said John with closed eyes and smiled softly as he was absorbed in his world.

"We tried our best to save these cities, but men, can only be controlled so much. At one point our planet was under a heavy burden of crime and insanity. When it went out of control the world quarters passed the bill to create skyscrapers, they were safe, more secured and built for the people who wanted to live their lives in peace and order. The rest of the society was buried underneath this city of Industries," said Pascal, as he didn't really talk to John but more to himself.

John came back to himself, took the headphone off and gasped for deep breath, "Is this really real Mr. Pascal, or is my son playing some joke with me?"

Pascal stayed quiet and didn't say a word for a while, then after a moment he spoke to John again.

"I am sure by now you've enjoyed the pleasure and fun of this incredible place, your tour shall continue as there isn't much time left before they arrive," said Pascal as he disappeared.

"Whose arrival?" asked John, while behind him was his car, which came inside the club.

Jack was speeding down the freeway in a peculiar vehicle with Pascal. He came across a mountain range. There, his point of view showed Aditya behind uniquely shaped purple mountains. The freeway was no normal Earthy looking road. Its vehicles were moving on an electric current generated on the ground below. The drivers were not driving the car next to him; the driver was sitting in the back as any normal passenger, reading newspapers or using digital interfaces.

Some of the cars on the freeway were completely transparent as everything from the passenger and the engineering inside could clearly be seen.

At the end of the freeway, a huge tunnel opened and was entirely white from the inside. Every single brick of the wall had a permanent white glow.

Jack, while moving, saw small glowing boxes on the ground on an isolated grassy area. When his car got near them, he saw a huge field of these rectangular shaped boxes, around hundreds and thousands of them, glowing from the bottom.

When he landed nearby, he witnessed unrecognizable symbols on the blocks. He walked across these things with curiosity. One would think of this place as a cemetery. It was remote, in a dark and lonely place. From the forest came a giant crane carrying steel boxes with bodies inside.

The steel box became transparent as human bodies were asleep in tranquility, after a few moments a ring of fire inside burned the body into ashes. This process took no more than ten seconds.

"Death, as it seems doesn't come without a sense of peace," said Pascal as again he walked in front of Jack.

"On the other hand we know what death is and what lies beyond the bounds of life. Everything has a motor or a main construct CPU with a timed clock. For us it's an invisible gas, which circulates through our body; by reading your fingerprints we could detect the timing of a person's death. Once the certain function stops in your body for more than 18.4 seconds this gas escapes and mixes with thin air. That gas doesn't carry your genes or genetic buildup but only carries your thoughts and knowledge; it's how you portray your image into this world. I will take you to a place that is quite unique but very much universal."

Pascal walked up to Jack, and looked him directly in the eyes with intensity.

"This particular gas, when exposed to the natural air gathers a mysterious matter which gives it the ability to go 400 million times faster than the speed of light, towards the dark side of this Universe, where it is in eternal peace. We proved this myth into a scientific reality about 300 years ago. We found out that this gas from our body actually enters two white gates. Yes, we saw a tiny blurred glimpse of these gates with our heavily advanced telescope hovering above the planet. It's a mysterious place where these souls live. And that's where we received our invitation from."

"This place is 1.3 trillion light years away from beyond the boundary of this Universe. Where you'll only witness nothing except darkness for a long time, but then you'll see them, two small glowing doors where these gases enter. We couldn't believe our eyes. We've seen everything, but this was something that went beyond our imagination. This is the place from where we received our invitation. We don't know what lies behind those gates. But we are going to find out."

Jack was pulling his hair bamboozled by what he was hearing at that moment. Pascal stood next to him looking at the view. On a small hill next to him was John, listening, while another Pascal was standing beside him.

"Come with me," he said as they both blasted into a white light which landed them in front of a small room.

Jack and Pascal walked inside the shop where an older man behind a desk was looking at some paperwork. In front of him sat a young bachelor.

On the paper was the exact same chart that, "Vedic Astrologers" used in North India.

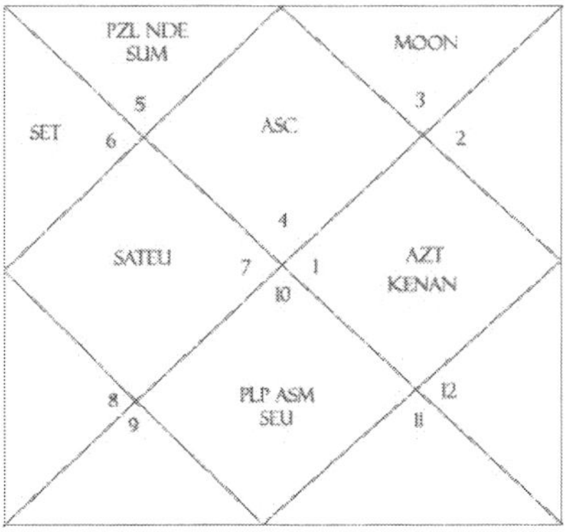

"Azc Nebula is looking over Setpulain planet which is sitting in the third house and this is why your marriage is being delayed. But not to worry, you'll meet her in 3 months but nothing before that. I will also add that your fortune will change once you marry her. But stay in the writing business, it will take you to new heights. Even though your ascendant lord is in the 12th house of loses, it will also give you unbelievable imagination and writing ability, you're a great storyteller. No writer becomes successful if they don't have any one of these planets in the 12th house. He also advised him to wear a blue stone named, "Killaphire," to balance his malefic planet energy.

"This is called "Inatic Astrology." This is not magic but celestial guidance and more accurate than science itself. Through the placement of planets in our constellations, we can determine the fate of a person's entire life, and what he or she will or will not achieve in their lifetime. It requires the time of birth and his date to make this diagram. This is not a hoax, the invisible rays of planets during a person's birth can determine the map of a person's life. Every single moment our planet emits different levels of radiation, vibration and cosmic rays from its inner core to the outer atmosphere. When a baby is exposed to these rays at the time of his or her birth, it will effect is subconscious level from that point on, and, the planets act as agents of those rays throughout the child's life. All celestial bodies are biological organisms, connected to ever single thing in this Universe. You must know one thing, without the energy of planetary alignment; nothing can be accomplished in one's life. There may be thousands more brilliant scientists like myself, but only because of my planetary strength, I was able to make to this elite society of intellects. In order to succeed in life, you must improve those bad and debilitated planets. But like us, you'll figure out its remedies. Goodbye my friend," said Pascal, as complete whiteness took over Jack's eyes.

Back on Earth Laura was getting anxious and looking at the clock with an overwhelming sense of anxiety. There was a silence in the basement, as John and Jack were stuck in the matrix of a parallel Universe.

Suddenly, the bodies inside the tube began to shake violently. The thick liquid type material started to evaporate.

Laura wiped her eyes and took a step towards the cylinder. Jack was the first one to be released from the glass, as he was slobbered in the thick sticky gel. He walked up to Laura feeling queasy and fatigued, while John was picking the gel from his body feeling indifferent and unaffected. He glanced at this son, shook his head in comedic disappointment, and kept on cleaning himself.

CHAPTER 8

THE CALM BEFORE THE STORM

Blurriness faded away from Jack's eyes as he lay in the bedroom covered in three layers of blankets. He slowly regained consciousness, opened his eyes, and saw Laura and kids standing next to him as he jittered from a lack of breathing.

"Hey dad, are you okay?" said Michael who was sitting right next to Jack.

"I am fine," said Jack as he slowly got up, while feeling a some acute pain in his back.

"Why is grandpa acting strange?" asked Lisa.

"What? Where is he?" Jack asked.

"He's in the basement, playing with your mathematic problem on the board," Laura replied in a calmly manner.

Jack quickly stood up from the bed, but held his back from the sudden pain. He gathered himself together and approached the kids. "Ok time for bed you guys."

"Bed? It's only seven in the evening," replied Laura.

"Oh," said Jack as he stood there a bit confused. He then realized his father was in the basement. He quickly rushed to the stairs while putting his slippers on.

"So how is dad?" asked Jack to Laura while in a rush.

"It would be better if you ask him yourself," she replied. Laura didn't want to give Jack a complete answer, as if she wanted him to figure it out on his own.

Dim light was facing towards the board where Jack's mathematical equation had been completed and modified by John. Sitting right in front of it without any expression on his face John kept his concentration on revising the problem. He didn't even move his eyes, but realized that Jack had entered the basement from the way his steps muttered on the wooden steps. They were slow and cautious.

"I can't believe the time frame either. Do you think I did this right?" asked John without even turning around and glancing at his son.

Jack came right next to him and said, "It's more accurate than life itself, and you actually gave this thing a soul."

"What is the possibility of two guys knowing about a five hundred year old computer buried beneath the surface of the Earth?" asked John.

"What is the possibility of two guys making a total ass of themselves after the time has expired of the planet to arrive, and not doing anything about it," replied Jack as he too stared at the board.

"Two in six billion," John replied without getting up or looking towards Jack.

"That's huge," Jack replied.

"Pascal told me something before he vanished from my sight inside the high club. He said, 'it's time for you to go now, before their arrival,' and then he disappeared," said John.

"Really?"

"This board had some major problems on it you know," said John.

"I kind of knew that, from the way I divided the mod FX and 88.3 powers to the third into DX," said Jack.

"You were suppose to subtract it not divide it genius," said John.

"I thought I'd use mom's old trick and think the other way when the mind couldn't find a solution," replied Jack as he glanced at his father.

"You owe me three hundred dollars," said John abruptly.

"What three hundred dollars?"

"I thought you weren't ever going to talk about mom again or you'll give me three hundred dollars," John replied.

John stayed quiet while looking at certain point in the basement.

"I wish you could've lived with me after she passed away," said Jack.

"Did you ever care to ask me? Without saying a single word, you left the house the next day, and for God's sake Jack I wasn't going to ask you to take me while you were dating Tracy. You were heartbroken, I was heartbroken. I could've used some company time to time you know. But I stayed quiet, I didn't say anything, because at the end, you're my blood and I knew keeping my distance is what you desired."

"You wouldn't have been thrilled anyway having me pick up two strange children from the street, without even thinking twice."

"Son, I respect you and admire you, but; if you say that kind of low life crap again, this seventy year old still has some strength in his fists. Just because that your mother nor I found it difficult to understand you for your first thirty years. That doesn't mean we gave up on you Jack. I know the odd kid you were, how isolated and egotistic you were regarding all your work. With or without criticism you stood your ground, because you are my blood and following what you believe in your DNA as well as your soul."

"Sorry dad, the past 4 years have been the oddest times of my life. I mean what guy picks up two random children off the street and brings them home? Most of them date and drink till they're gray."

"I figured that one out a long time ago son. I know you wanted to nurture someone completely differently than way you were raised, and I know Tracy wasn't going to let you do that, with her ego being involved."

"I want to ask you something dad? I was a little hesitant about it in the past but this is just an odd situation between us."

"What's the question?"

Jack stayed quiet for a moment, trying to think of how to put words together, and communicate with his father in a manner which wouldn't erupt into a redundant argument.

"Why was I so misunderstood between you and mom?"

"Because you are different, you are a genius, and it is hard understanding someone who surpasses your own intelligence and ideas from an early age. Christ, I can't believe what the hell has been going on for the past 36 hours. Pack up your stuff, yours and the children," said John.

He went straight to the conclusion without properly answering his son's question. John couldn't wait any longer and he couldn't stand seeing his son and grandchildren living in such conditions.

"What?" Jack asked while looking directly at him.

In a very serious tone John answered back.

"You guys are moving in with me first thing in the morning, I am not going to miss a second of my grandchildren growing up, especially not in this rotten hell place you call home. Say what you want but I am taking my son and grandchildren tomorrow."

Jack thought for a minute while John kept talking to him about his inner emotions. "I don't know what you're thinking about but I am not going to let you talk me out of this, I am not leaving unless your ass comes with me," said John.

Jack still didn't say anything, but he was absorbed in this own thoughts.

"Say something for God's sake; I can use a good fight right now to get my heart started."

Jack still stayed silent to what seemed like an aging father giving up on a rare conversation with his son.

"You have to clean the bathtub though, I can't stand your hair near the drain," said Jack.

John glanced and smiled at him.

"As you can tell, I don't have much hair left, but I'll do my best son," replied John.

"I can't put Michael and Lisa through this, there is no reason for them to walk down this path due to my ego and foolishness, as much as I want to say no, I know I can't. My room is still the same right?" asked Jack knowing clearly well what he was about to get into.

"Down to the last smelly underwear hanging on your chair," replied John.

"My God, for a minute I forgot what we have with us in this basement," said Jack.

"Same here, which tells you something, that emotions and love hold stronger meaning than the discovery of intergalactic aliens," John replied.

Both glanced towards the silent computer, where a small red key was lit.

"Why is that key lit?" John asked.

"Don't know," Jack got up and walked towards the computer. He reached the device and observed the button.

"I am going to press it," said Jack.

"What the hell are you waiting for?" replied John.

Jack pressed the button as the computer came back to life, and the white screen popped up again with Pascal sitting in front of the camera.

"I hope you've enjoyed and learned from your journey to my world. Whether it still exists or not, I hope it has given a light to you and your people to keep searching and keep looking for life beyond your boundaries. Because there are at least three possibilities we know of that might exist in your solar system and a planet 97 light years away from your star system. Our mission was not to give you a guided tour of a new world, but to warn you."

"Not every alien race is friendly and not every alien race is deadly. By the time your world gets developed into intelligent supreme beings, we believe Spastic-9, a planet about 96.346 light years away which lay behind a thick black cloud of gas, will be nine times more advance than you, and will likely try to either make contact or may come in person.

"There is no sunlight on that planet, but the planet is an energy maker in itself. The way it's built; it won't require a star or natural satellite. I am really curious to see what these creatures will look like knowing there is no source of light, but in our scientific studies we have come to one conclusion; when something or someone doesn't have what others are using for survival, this Universe provides them with a unique tool to live just like the rest. I cannot stress enough to say this but the Universe is alive. It knows your every move; it knows what you're thinking and sees everything. Your life depends upon the mercy of this Universe, it may not sink in right now but the Universe does breathe, have eyes and has a working, thinking brain. We saw this in person."

John while watching the screen spoke to Jack, "He's on to something."

Pascal glanced at the screen for about six seconds then continued his speech.

"I have to apologize to you and your race for a tiny mistake I always make, in hopes of an intelligent life to evolve in a distant future. But it's a necessary mistake where a chance has to be taken. The device that you found underneath the surface has a tracking chip; as soon as it turns on by the touch of a living being the ultra laser signal will be sent out to Planets closest to you, which are intelligent enough to understand such signals. The signal will reach that planet in approximately one hour from the time you hear this message."

Pascal had guilt showing on his face with his head down in shame. He knew an intelligent life would be viewing this at some point. He then slowly glanced back at the camera while taking a deep breath.

"They are coming."

The computer turned off as Laura was standing behind John and Jack. All three of them were just standing still not saying a word.

Laura's eyes were wet, but no tear was dropping down. But softly she took a crying breath. John and Jack heard it and looked back.

Jack went up to Laura, and held her in his arms.

"Kids can't know about this, ok. They cannot. Tomorrow morning we are going to my dad's house. I don't know who and if I am going to contact anyone, but right now I want you to be strong."

Laura kept looking into Jack's eyes as a tear fell out, as she agreed with Jack's request.

"We don't even know if something will come within an hour, this, um, this computer could be defective."

"That will really help her, Jackass," said John as he got up and came near Laura and took her in his arms.

"Honey, what you are a part of is going to be written in the history books of not just this planet, but other planets alike. Your name and believe me when I say this, your name will be on a much higher platform than Neil Armstrong or Dr. Jack Crawford. Other girls like you would die to be a part of something like this, and Jack knows he can't live without you, and you without him, so I am going to accept you as my daughter right now because, well because," John kept silent as he didn't know what he wanted to say next to this innocent, honest and beautiful woman. Perhaps she was a new symbol of true love and commitment after his late wife.

"Tomorrow may not come," said Laura and finished what John really wanted to say from within.

"Well now, let's not jump to such drastic conclusions. I was just trying to say, there is no one in this world that can take care and give love to Michael and Lisa other than you." John after giving his complete love and support to Laura realized they must all be together, at all times. They all agreed to John's request, it was a choice that didn't need any thinking.

Laura wiped her tears off then gave John a hug.

"Thank you so much, dad," replied Laura as she softly punched John on his chest, and a smile appeared on her face.

"What do you think?" John asked.

"I wish I could think right now. I don't know how I am holding my hands from not picking up the phone and calling everyone," replied Jack.

"Come with me," said John as he started walking upstairs.

"Come, come," he repeated again.

Jack without saying anything followed John, "wait," replied Jack as he quickly walked down and took the computer cart and rolled it over to his safe box and closed its door.

Jack closed the light of the basement and walked back upstairs.

John put on his coat, which was hanging behind the main door.

"Where we going?" asked Jack.

"Just wear something warm, will yaa, It's snowing for God sake." John replied and walked outside side the house. Jack followed, while quickly grabbing his jacket and gloves.

"What is this all about dad?"

"Get in the car," said John as he got inside his car.

Jack was confused about this whole trip.

"What? You want to go to strip bar or get hookers?"

John's car pulled up in front of Snow Angles a strip bar about twenty miles from Jack's house.

"Oh you're not kidding," said Jack as he got his head cleared about the confusion. The car stopped as both of them sat and stared at the bar without saying a word. After a few moments, Jack spoke back to his father.

"So, you want to ring the bell or should I?" asked Jack.

"It's party time," said John, with a glow on his face and a smile that Jack had witnessed in past. Jack never really understood his father, but never went against his innocent wishes either. He knew they were harmless in comparison to the world.

The club was crowded with young and middle aged men, watching strippers in bikinis dancing on the pole. There were some young crowds in front of the club in a huge group, screaming and throwing their dollar bills on stage.

Jack as usual was sitting at the bar drinking. There were some people sitting next to him that had their eyes locked on the stage. A strange man next to Jack took a whole shot in one take, then asked him a question. "You're like the only guy with his back to the stage, you sure you at the right place?"

"Seen it a million times, just need a good drink that's all, but my dad seems to be enjoying it," replied Jack.

"Where is he?"

Among the group of young men holding dollar bills in their hand was John Crawford celebrating life with a smile, enjoying as if it was his last day on Earth. The stripper came down to his level as he put a dollar bill in his mouth and gave it to the stripper. He howled in delight as the stripper danced her way onto his lap.

A couple of hours later, father and son decided to grab some food. They both ended up at a fried chicken place named "Louie's wings," down at the corner of downtown. They were both indulging in nitpicking each and every bone of the chicken. John picked up the hot sauce and sprayed it on Jack's plate.

"More?" John asked.

"Oh yeah," replied Jack.

"Good huh…?"

"Love it, even though it's nothing close to what we ate earlier, but right now this is what Philly is all about. Jack took a huge bite from the chicken leg. "Dad I want you to know, if we come-out of this safe and sound, I want you to be with me for life. I guess I need to thank Pascal for making this happen."

"But I am proud of you at this moment, especially for the last ten seconds," said John.

"Explain professor," Jack replied.

"You actually put the matter of love and family before this Universe, you forgot for a second what has happened in the last 2 days; that has changed everything for this planet. The world just doesn't know it yet," said John.

"It's kind of like the Wright brothers thing huh, only 30 people knew about a flying plane for more than a week, before it took the world by storm. But dad, just don't tell anyone about this, please."

The restaurant was practically empty as only one older couple was eating. John loudly blubbered out to the cashier "hey, we're going to be attacked by aliens in about two hours, as we found a five hundred million year old computer in the ground."

A Mexican cashier with front teeth missing just smiled and continued his dusting.

"See, no one gives a crap. I can't even believe it, I have to convince myself!" said John.

"Laura can use some help, we'll make her the star," replied Jack.

"I guess she can be it, by the way, how did you meet this nice lady? Tell me about her," John asked.

"She is a bartender down the street from where I work, well used to work. When I visited the bar for the first time she was actually trying to study for her biology exam while serving me drinks, and that's how it all began."

"And you started helping her by hitting on her."

"I never said I was hitting on her… ok I was, a little. First night I met her was on Michael's 4th birthday, we were coming back from the play house as I decided to grab a quick drink, but it was a Tuesday night and the place was practically dead at that time. We just talked the night away. Man, the even the kids had a good time with her that night, it was the first time they all met, and it all just came together so well. I remember she came to my house and put them to sleep. Lisa refused to leave her arms that night."

"Jack, a beautiful woman like that who loves kids and cooks great Italian food is bigger than having mutual funds."

"Yeah, I know."

"Took you long enough time to see it though," said John.

"How do you know that?"

"We were talking while you were knocked out from your adventure today."

"I just didn't want the love for the kids to be divided," said Jack.

"Not bad for a jackass, talking to that young girl for thirty minutes felt like I was talking to mom again," said John in a playfully angry manner. "You don't know, you don't know! How much that woman loves you, and you know why, for nothing. She just fell in love Jack, unconditionally. It's not some bullhorn love that one creates after marrying a rich person. Right now she's home mothering your kids like they need to be. What the hell are you doing? Tell me? A woman like that throws herself at you, and you can't seem to give a second of attention to her. Screw science and education if a man doesn't even know how to appreciate a good woman."

Jack's tears started flowing without a cause, as he tried to look elsewhere and avoid paying attention to John.

"What the hell is the matter with you? You're testing her if she's worthy of getting married, shame on you son."

"I am a screw-up, always have been, but my ego just went too far this time. I just didn't think a woman like that would be able to cope with my lifestyle," replied Jack.

"Lifestyle!, Jack is there drug dealing going on, are there drug dealers, gang members hanging around your house, are you making minimum wage, even as a construction worker you're making $25 dollars an hour, you have a Masters and a Ph.D. Don't give me that nonsense about testing her, you are just afraid, you are afraid of losing that girl, and that's the only reason. You know you love her, yet you haven't got the sense of adoring her. She is God to you Jack. I know this is not the time to talk about such a personal and sensitive subject but that woman had tears when she was talking about how much she loves you and the kids. You are the only family for her, she has no mother or father, no siblings, and her relatives don't like her. I want to slap you silly right now."

A realization awoke within Jack. He was quite an acute schizophrenic when it came to love and relationships. It was a mind game to him. But a few wise and hard words from his father gave him a clear picture.

"That's it, I don't care if anyone else is ready or not, tomorrow morning I am marrying Laura," Jack told his father as he got up and exited the restaurant.

John followed, but took a quick last bite of chicken leg as he left the table.

Jack glanced up at the sky as he walked to the car and stopped. John, who was right behind him also halted and looked up at the sky as well. And for a while, they didn't say anything to each other, but then John spoke. "What is it?" he asked Jack. "Stars are kind of bright tonight, actually really bright," replied Jack.

"You're right, but it's strange, clouds are all over the place," said John, but then Jack points to the sky "look dad, they are bright enough to be showing from behind the clouds, strange."

There was a small tree next to John, he held one of the leaves from the tree, smelled it and treated it like his pet. He then looked around the city with more detail, observed people walking around, the lights of the street that were flickering time to time and the houses that existed around the area. It was nothing special, nor did it hold any beauty, but when a man knows this could be his last day living, even the dirt seems more valuable.

John grabbed Jack from his back and hugged him. Jack couldn't understand the reason for the hug but he went with the flow and hugged his father back.

"I think this might be the only wish that will come true in my lifetime," said John.

"What are you talking about dad? We don't even know if they are coming, we don't know if they are going to be hostile or friendly, now let's go home, you need to be with your grandkids and daughter in-law."

Jack smiled at his father as John softly slapped him on the cheek. They both got into the car and drove home.

The car pulled up in front of the house as Laura watched from the window. Jack noticed her pretty face and rushed out of the car and ran towards the house. Laura came to the door as Jack tightly grabbed her and kissed her passionately.

"Ok, I am sorry but this is not your house, you must have mistaken this for something else," said Laura to Jack.

"I love you, yes, I love you, I love you more than anything else, sorry for doing this to you the entire time. I love you! Laura I love you and tomorrow we will get married, no one deserves you but me."

Laura looked into Jack's eyes for awhile, and then suddenly had tears rolling down her cheeks. She quietly rested her head on his chest. John watched the couple in peace from outside. They both stood still under a tiny dim light hanging above them. A moment John only knew in the past, with his late wife. John looked on...and then saw himself as a young man with his wife in their first house, dancing on the porch.

The moment was so precious that no one would have wanted it to end. The present John stood at the door looking at his young self-dissolved into pure love with his late beautiful wife.

He quickly woke from this daydream and walked over to Laura who stood at the door waiting for him to come inside.

"Hurry up dad, its freezing out there," said Laura.

John looked on with love towards Laura and said, "You've earned the right to call me that honey."

As he walked into the house, John noticed that the time read 11:00 pm.

"Now how about we all get some sleep, or at least try to?" said John while he hung his jacket on the hook. Jack glanced at him and agreed. They all quietly faded into the dark hallway. A tiny glimpse of a green laser shot out from the side of Jack's basement and the action lasted no more than half a second. The laser shot itself into the endless sky towards an undisclosed location.

John slept deeply, so much so that his snore echoed loudly in the room. On the bed were John, Lisa, Laura, and

Michael. On the other corner was Jack whose eyes were open. Behind him there was a window that showed a full moon and other stars, which were shining brighter than usual. He stared at them upside down. He slowly turned around and put his hand under his chin on the edge of the window. The room was getting a blue glow from the nightlight of the moon and the street.

Jack seemingly stared at one particular star, which was blinking brighter than the others. Slowly Jack began to get sleepy as his eyes began to open and closed rapidly. He turned around and looked at the clock, which reads 11:45 PM.

The star that was blinking bright in the sky got bigger by the second and then, suddenly, it disappeared into the dark night.

NSC

HUSTON, TEXAS

A dim light was lit in the main frame area of NSC, as only one or two scientists were sitting working with three cups of coffee on their desk, and an ashtray which hadn't been cleaned in weeks.

Clark Gabriel, one of the lead scientists at NSC and a former friend of Jack was working on a super computer at his desk. He had very short army cut hair and cheekbones strongly showing on his face. He looked around the age of 40 or perhaps mid 40's with a perfectly healthy body. As he sat around and watched a monitor with radio wave signals, another man came with a cup of coffee and sat next to him.

Tom Saluki, one of the lunar scientists working on the Mars project, was an avid late worker at NSC like Clark.

"Aren't you going home soon?" said Tom as he sipped on his coffee and relaxed on the chair.

"Life is much better hanging around this mouse hole," replied Clark as he took a hit of his cigarette.

"Heard about the division C being laid off?" asked Tom.

"Yeah, found out from Jim this morning; vouchers give zero support. Its better being laid-off than to work on the razors edge every day, sometimes I feel like doing what Jack did when he left, at least he had his chin-up instead of being bent over."

"Yeah, yeah, the one who was predicting the invisible planet, about 80 thousand miles away from Pluto, What happened to him?"

"He's down in Philadelphia somewhere, don't know what he's up to but the kid was a genius. That's why they got rid of the expensive lamb to bring in the cheap goat. This corporation could've done wonders Tom, now here we are listening to people's washing machines all night long."

"At least you're still getting your weekly paycheck," replied Tom.

"Are you're kidding me? I don't go home because I'll save money on my electric bill. Anyways, that kid had some method to his madness, his dad is a genius too, teaches at University Of Pennsylvania. And you know it's just not him, there have been fifteen of those guys that came and passed by," said Clark.

"I remember one time; Jack told me that building a spaceship of diamond will lower the risk of getting burned during take-off and reentry to .001%. The whole board laughed that day, I don't know, for some reason it made sense. You see, those are the kind of people we need, not a bunch of corporate heads running around on the table going by the book. There is no independent thinking anymore in any field; they shut you up with the dollars. I swear if I were half a genius, I wouldn't dog myself about this right now. You know why, because I would be out on my own."

"Sometimes I think if I even belong in this place, I feel so isolated in this organization. I am ready to go work for Paul Allen's agency right now I'll tell you that. You know they already announced a mission to Pluto, all we keep chasing here is a metal cardboard box on red sand," said Clark.

"I actually had a meeting with Graff a couple of days ago, they want two guys for data analysis on the Europa project, I can mention your name if you want?" said Tom.

"Yes, yes, please do, geez, thank you Tom, the best things happen to you in the middle of the night." replied Clark.

"And the worst," replied Tom as he smiled.

"Come out with me, I got more smokes in the car," said Clark as both men got up and walked out of the room and into the open night sky.

Clark glanced up at the stars.

"Geez, the stars are awfully bright tonight."

"Yeah, you're right."

Both of them walked away towards the parking lot while smoking. "Bernanke is another joke to this country, keeps bringing down the value of the dollar every time there is a panic. I mean what's the reason for lowering rates every time the market goes down 300 points, next thing you know, you can't even buy a cheeseburger in Europe with your dollar."

"Actually you can't anymore, it's like 4 pounds for a cheeseburger there," replied Tom.

Tom and Clark walked inside the building while still talking, a couple of guards stood in the front of the gate. Tom and Clark shook hands with both of them.

CHAPTER 9

THE ARRIVAL

Silence roared onto the quiet street of Jack's neighborhood while a few streetlamps were lit and flickered rapidly. No human being was visible in any direction. A slow gust of wind moved a couple of papers and dry leaves lying on the street, as a bit of fog had appeared due to the cold weather.

The wind was creaking the window of Jack's house where all five of them were sleeping on single bed. At the moment, even a pin drop could be heard in the house. Time stood still. The ticking of the clock's pin was loudly heard.

In this quiet moment, a very deep thump echoed all across town as Jack opened his eyes. He looked straight on without moving a single hair on his body. Another thump fluttered the walls. Jack's eyebrows went up. He rose up from the bed but didn't look towards the window. John, too, had his eyes opened as he turned around and glanced towards Jack, who was sitting up on his bed looking at the wall.

"What was that?" asked John.

Jack got up slowly as another thump occurred. Laura woke up in fright.

"Stay with the kids, I'll be back," whispered Jack as he gazed into Laura's eyes. John followed him in the back. "I am coming with you", he said, while Michael and Lisa remained asleep, as Laura's gentle hand came and rubbed on their hair. She curiously looked up at the sky but couldn't seem to find anything strange.

Jack rushed downstairs, as he quickly tried to wear his jacket. John followed him in his sleeping suit and a hat with a woolen ball hanging by a thread. Another thump occurred, as if someone had slammed a huge stone on a mound of dirt.

Jack rushed outside the house. On the street, other families were coming out and looking for a source of the sound. On the other side of the street more people were coming out from their houses looking towards the sky.

"Hey Jack what's going on?" yelled his neighbor across the street. "I don't know must be an Earthquake," Jack yelled back as he came in the middle of the street followed by his dad. There was nothing in the sky and nothing in both directions.

The thump occurred again, but this time everyone heard it from one direction, from behind the hill.

"They are here," said John as he came close to Jack.

"Jesus," replied Jack in a soft tone.

All the people came together slowly on the street. There were even children on people's shoulders and arms.

The sound occurred very close to the area, as all the people slowly started to move back, but even now nothing was visible.

Above the Earth's orbit was a Russian space station where two astronauts were working and talking on the phone with Russian intelligence; telling them about a strange signal they witnessed couple of hours ago.

"At this time we do confirm the signal but there is no visibility of any object, the signal appeared on the system at 21:06:42, but again I confirm there is no visibility of an object at this time, copy."

Inside the NSC center, Clark spoke aggressively on the telephone calling everyone and screaming on the phone, "I don't have the damn time to tell you all the details. It came in three hours ago. I've been calling everyone for the last twenty minutes you moron, just get your ass over here!" Clark hung up and again started calling another number. After the first ring he was getting frustrated, "come on, come on answer you fat pig, what the hell, what the hell, come on," said Clark to himself.

"This is Terry," said the man on the other line.

"Terry, don't ask questions, don't scratch your ass just come over right now, we have a 201, I repeat, we got a 201."

Clark hung up, while Tom walked across him on the phone talking to his superior, "it came in three and a half hours ago and I just confirmed with the space-station. It's on the 26 longitude, everyone is coming over, and I even got the damn janitors helping on the phone."

(In Spanish) "maami this is Alajandro, how is paapi doing? I just got promoted from a cleaning person to a rocket scientist. Yes mammi, I am so happy," said the janitor helping Clark and Tom out on the call list. The room was filled with 10 other scientists.

The parking lot of NSC was getting cramped up with cars. Scientist ran into the building in over coats, sleeping suits, pajamas, with kids and babies in their arms.

The crowd rushed into the building as if it were a reverse fire drill. The men and women came running into the main deck, rushed to their desk and computers and began logging on. One of the female scientists grabbed the phone from the janitor and told him to get out.

Around Clark there were four older men aged 45-60, as Mark Walls listened to Clark describing the signal. "After adding up the above numbers the major part of the signal came in the Earth's range around eighteen hundred hours, but the transmitter didn't catch the wave till 21 0 6, but this is where you start scratching your head. This is the grand finale folks. An unidentified signal left the Earth at 1700 straight, 88 degree at 125 latitude. Even the military and Pentagon can't identify its nature and location at this point, but their boys are working on it. After the strange signals left Earth in that direction, towards the Erickson Nebula, this new strange signal came back from the same location in no less than three hours but..."

"But what?" asked Mark. "I don't think it is just a signal sir," said Clark. "Then, what the hell is it?" Mark asked, "It sounds like an object sir," replied Clark.

"You're kidding me," said John Finch one of the men standing next to him. "Can we confirm that from the outer source?" said Mark.

"I just did sir," replied Clark.

"Did they see anything up there?"

"No, they did not, but the U.S submarine's radar caught an unseen object for no less than one second. This is why I think, whatever it is, it is fast and it's advanced."

"What the hell is going on?" asked Mark as he looked into everyone's eye.

"There're here," said Clark.

Everyone stared at each other. Then, Mark called everyone to the boardroom. "Let's set up the conference call with the White House in the next ten minutes, and get me the CIA and FBI chief as well on the call," said Mark to John Finch. All four of the senior executives walked away.

"You want me to called Ronald as well sir?" said Clark to the walking executives, as they were about to exit the room. "We'll take care of that," replied Mark.

Jack and rest of the people in the area looked towards the sky from the window. By now the sky was glowing pink in the late night. The clouds gave the color of a very mystic ambience; one can get a feeling that something very strange was about to happen.

On the main streets of Philadelphia the traffic was jammed as passengers and drivers were standing outside their cars looking at the sky. The thumping sound now turned into the sound of a machine gearing up to perform an action. People searched for the sound in all directions.

On the street, a big rig was parked in a diagonal direction blocking more than ¾'s of the highway. People were confused as to what was happening. All the cell phones died. The people tried to make calls but couldn't get through.

Behind the highway was a forest, where wolves had come out onto the edge howling, as the people were in panic not knowing what to do. They were looking in the back at these massive numbers of wolves and on the other hand this strange noise was taking their attention away.

Laura and the kids were also getting ready to go out on the street as she put warm clothes on them.

"What's happening?" asked Lisa, while still half asleep as she rubbed her eyes.

"Nothing honey, we might be going on a trip, that's all," Laura replied.

"I want to go too," said Michael, as he got anxious.

"Yes, we are going there, now come on wear your jacket Michael."

In the same block, more people piled up. The amount went from twenty to thirty and now to into the hundreds. Jack and John observed the attention this phenomenon was getting.

The people were jammed onto the street as they looked ahead to the hilltop.

"The message," said Jack to himself as he ran back into the house.

"Where are you going?" said John, as he followed behind him.

Laura was coming down with the kids as she saw Jack storming to the basement.

"What's going on?" asked Laura to Jack.

"Just follow me and you'll find out yourself."

Laura with the kids came downstairs, while Jack was taking the computer out from the locked cabinet.

Jack noticed everyone especially the kids. He looked at them for a few seconds but continued turning the computer on.

He turned KYIRUX on from the main power, as the entire button flashed at once, but then, he started looking for the button he was suppose to push. All the lights stayed lit in the same manner. Then, from below the machine, another keyboard came out. On the keyboard, there were two red keys lit. Jack glanced back at Laura, "I think you might want to cover their eyes for this," said Jack, as Laura put her hands over both Lisa and Michael.

Jack pressed the button and again the white light appeared, fading out to the outside view of Earth 500 million years ago, where Pascal and his team were gathered together.

The ship was in a much different shape, more like a building with a nuclear plant under construction.

Pascal was speaking to his crew in concern.

"How much longer?" said Pascal.

"Another two hours," replied Lava as she caught her breath, perhaps she ran to him, to give him certain news.

"I suggest we get the ship back to launching position, and let's start drilling for the rocks," commanded Pascal.

Lava and Calculus understood and ran back inside the ship.

Pascal reached to his talking device as he sent a message off to Lava, "Get the GNX box from the 56 cabin."

Lava running at this time stopped and glances towards Calculus as they both realize what Pascal was asking for.

Pascal on the other hand put the video pen on a rock and gave another message. "I will have to depart soon from your planet, but I shall leave you a gift which I hope you'll make good use of.

"I will be leaving a box of..."

The message interrupted, as the thump occurred again outside. The lights of the house went out and the computer shutoff.

"Dad, Laura," called Michael in the darkness.

"Yes, yes, I am here, hold my hand baby," said Laura.

"Alright, nobody panic. I am here you guys, ok. I am slowly stepping back," said Jack as he stepped back in the dark.

John looked around in the opposite direction while Jack was stepping closer and closer, and suddenly, they both bumped into each other as John screamed.

"Dad, it's me.," whispered Jack.

"Oh good, I thought it was the aliens."

"Alright, alright, now let's move upstairs slowly," said Jack.

"Can I hold you son?" said John as he grabbed his shirt.

Jack just shook his head and started moving upstairs with Laura and the kids, while John followed behind him taking short quick steps.

"You know dad, you need to start dating again."

"He does not, he's doing fine without one. Don't re-marry Mr. John, it's not well for your health," replied Laura.

"I agree, that's why I go to Angles," John asked.

Jack looked at his father, gave him a dirty look and poked him in the stomach.

"Oh right, right, we're not suppose to talk about It," said John.

"You went to Angles didn't you just now?" questioned Laura, in a whispering and quiet manner to Jack.

All five of them came upstairs as the reflection of cell phones and flashlights from the street were giving a fluorescent view of the outside streets.

Jack and the rest of the family came out of the house. At the end of the street, men were carrying flashlights and heading towards the hill. Joining them were policemen, firemen, doctors, insurance salesmen and your average American citizens.

The men were looking behind the rocks, digging in the dirt as they were trying to trace the sound of the machine, which sounded like it was throwing out steam.

"Do you know where the flashlight is Laura?" asked Jack as his eyes were locked on the hill.

"Why? You're going to leave us? I don't think so," Laura replied.

"Yeah, you're going to leave us? Sure as hell not me, because I am coming with you," John told everyone.

"I am going with Grandpa," Michael spoke and went over to John's side.

"Yeah, ok sure, get the flash light," said Jack as his full attention and concentration was still towards the hill.

"Hey, how come he gets to go? I want to go to," said Lisa as she looked into Laura's eyes.

"Who said we couldn't go? Of course we'll go," Laura replied.

Somehow Jack heard Laura talking to Lisa and replied back "no, you guys stay here. There are no women or children on the hill."

"No women or children my foot. Try stopping us," Laura said as she stormed off with Lisa towards the hill, while walking away, Jack yelled.

"I think you might need a flash light," said Jack.

"We already got one," Laura replied as she took out a flashlight from her left jacket pocket and turned it on.

Jack looked and felt like a fool, and then glanced at Michael and John, "I can't believe I am about to marry her."

"Alight follow the lady," as all three of them quickly ran and caught up with Laura.

"What do you think you will accomplish by putting yourself in danger and not to mention putting our children in the middle of it?" Jack abruptly stopped and realized what he just said. Laura came to a halt as well. She looked into his eyes knowing he just gave her the right to his children.

Laura stared into his eyes for a short bit, then, softly smiled and walked away.

Jack stood there pondering what he just said. From the back John tapped Jack, while holding Michael in his arms. "Ok, you'll be marrying Laura in two days, quit fantasizing about her, now let's move."

John dragged Jack towards the hill as Lisa and Laura were ahead of them. The sound of steam became loud at this time.

"Can I at least hold the flash light," said Jack as he walked aside Laura.

"Why? You think woman aren't capable of holding a flash light?"

"No, what I meant to say is that since you're holding Lisa it'll make it easier if we both shared the load, okay."

Laura gladly handed Lisa to Jack, "Now we can both share our work load, cool?"

Jack looked at Lisa and asked her a question while walking behind Laura.

"You like this mother?"

"She's the best, best, ever," replied Lisa.

"We love her don't we?" Jack said to Lisa as they caught up with Laura again.

"Slowdown you two," said John coming from behind.

"Grandpa you're fat," Michael told John, as they tried to catch up with Jack.

"Oh yeah… your dad smells like broccoli," replied John to Michael.

Jack and Laura kept walking for awhile. Then, Jack turned around, and saw no sign of John and Michael.

"Hold up, where is dad and Michael?" said Jack as he held Laura's shoulder.

"Wait, weren't they behind us."

"What the hell…" Jack began scanning the crowd.

Lisa suddenly spoke, "there they are, at the hotdog stand," as Lisa pointed her finger towards where John and Michael were stuffing their mouths with hotdogs.

"Oh Jesus," said Jack as they all went back.

"Hey what the hell is this? Put more onions on that man," said John as he took a sip of the soda, while Michael was still trying to get his first hotdog down.

While having a hotdog in his mouth Michael saw Jack and said, "Dad, have a hotdog."

John, while stuffing a hotdog in his mouth, glanced over to Jack and Laura.

"What? I was hungry," said John, as he saw Jack coming towards him with anger.

Jack stared at him for a while, then, suddenly changed his personality as he too asked the man at the stand to make him two chilidogs with extra onions.

"I don't want one," said Laura.

"Oh, I was actually taking it for myself," Jack replied while Laura slapped him on the shoulder.

"What? They have fried onions, come on," replied Jack.

"Its 11 o clock in the night and you're having this junk food," said Laura.

"But they have fried onions," replied Jack.

John on the other-hand gave a good burp, as he put his fist on his chest.

"Oh this was good," said John while wiping off his mouth.

Jack got his hotdog and stuffed it in his mouth like a pig. He then glanced over to Laura who just shook her head and left for the hill.

While having the hotdog stuffed in his mouth Jack spoke, "wait, hold on," he replied while running back.

Across the world in India a normal family was watching the news, while eating lunch at the table. The mother was in the kitchen baking the bread, as three kids and their father were busy eating and drinking. On the news there was a cricket match review going on. The son was cheering as he saw his favorite player hit the winning run.

"Oh man, he hit that, yes…" said the boy.

"I knew it, they had to give the ball to him, otherwise the whole team would've been out by this time," father replied as he watched the screen.

"Who wants more bread?" asked the mother in the kitchen.

"I'll take one, but I want rice as well," replied one of the two daughters sitting at the dining table with her head turned towards the T.V. After the match the news announcer went back to talking about the politics and what was happening in the parliament that week.

The family went back to finishing the dinner.

"Shalini told me you got a D in your math test?" said the father as he looked towards his 12-year-old son.

"I didn't get a D, it was C, I spoke to the teacher after school," his son replied.

"I don't care. You better get your ass going young man, and no more watching cricket, until I see a B or an A…"

Before the father could finish up the sentence the T.V. lost its signal, as the screen had color bars on them with a beeping sound. "Signal lost," appeared on the television screen.

The father picked up the remote and tried changing the channel, but every single channel was showing the same thing.

"This God damn company is going to be the death of me. I am going to cancel this crap tomorrow morning. I swear I am so tired of this crap," said the father.

"I've been telling you to get the satellite for the past two months; you can watch new movies as well. You know the people in flat 152, they watch everything new when it's in the theater?" said the mom.

"Hold on, let me call Malhotra." The father dialed the number to his friend.

"Hey Malhotra, I just wanted to know if your T.V was working?" said the father.

"I was just about to come to your place since I have this crap old cable. So, none of your channels are working?" replied Malhotra.

"No, they just went out all of a sudden. Even the dish company is trying to figure out what's going on."

Moving to different corners of the world; the same situation was happening as people in China, Japan, Europe, Africa, Middle East were trying to fix their television sets. All the people on the streets, across the world were talking and discussing about what was happening with cell phones and television stations. Electronic shops were filled with customers and people screaming and yelling at salesmen. Flights were being canceled all over the world due to no-radio connection between the craft and the tower.

In Italy, a restaurant was screening a soccer game on their television, when it suddenly lost single. Fear and paranoia was felt between people. An old man went crazy and began screaming while pulling his hair. The rest began yelling at the restaurant owner; who whispered to his wife to grab the gun.

Some radios were working around the world, as the Malhotra family and the others around their building had their ears locked on. The broadcaster was speaking in an urgent manner.

"All around the world communication is failing. Hardly any news is traveling across the globe at this time. All this chaos started about three hours ago when NSC scientist Clark Gabriel detected a strange signal from outer space. Now the world is in wonder of this mysterious fall out. Is the end near, or a sign of world war three? We can only pray and find out soon enough," said the radio host.

The radio started to lose its frequency and reception as the voice got distorted as the radio played a continuous beeping sound.

Indian Space Center, Kerela, India

Jay Michael Verma sat still on his desk in a very dark room. He stared at something in the reading glass without a blink. Scanning the board with an unsolved mathematical equation, Jay let out smoke from the cigarette that sizzled off his lips. He held his head with his left hand. In a matter of seconds he quickly got up and started jotting down numbers and symbols into the mathematical equation on the board. Once the equation was completed, Jay became terrified. He held his head with both his hands and began to step-back. He then said one word as he stormed out of the dark room.

"Jack..."

The ISC operates much the same way as NSC. Jay went right up the director of operation Aadesh Srivastava who was a very strong and tall personality. He listened to his scientist talking about the situation in an isolated place.

"Sir, sir," Jay came yelling towards him as Aadesh turned around.

"What happened?" he asked.

"I need to contact Jack Crawford, by any means possible," Jay replied.

"Are you going to tell me what the hell is going on?"

"I solved it. I solved it and it's not good, well I don't know actually, it's…it's complicated."

"What the hell do you mean? I told you before to stop wasting your time on that useless clutter. It's okay to do it during your lunch time, but we have more important things to do."

"One glance at his equation and it made sense sir, it just made sense, and I've solved it. There is no time to explain, I need to get in touch with Jack. He's the only one who can answer more questions regarding it," replied Jay.

"Oh, okay. Why don't I just give him a ring? Oh wait, the cell phones are not working, and neither have I had any clue about where Jack is after he left NSC. I suggest you find an alternative about your problem and it would be even wiser idea to help on this immediate situation."

"Sir, at this time, I am ready to ride on your back to go where he is. Just do something, fly me there, whatever you think; I just need to get in touch with Jack. He is in Philadelphia as far as I know," said Jay.

"Can I ask you something?" Aadesh asked.

"What?"

"What is the importance of this matter that you cannot even tell your own boss? And on top of that, commanding flights as if you're my superior. If it wasn't for that brain of yours, I would've had you kicked out 4 years ago from this facility. You're willing to go across the world to work for a White American, like two billion other Indians."

"Because bosses like you steal the original ideas of hard working white Americans like Jack, who devote their whole lives to something which you claim in a split second, anything else I can help you with, or should I just give my resignation right now." said Jay as he turned around, walked back and exited the room. "I don't give a damn anymore. I am done with you and this agency!" he yelled as he opened the door.

Aadesh saw everyone looking at him.

"Everyone back to work."

As Jay walked away from the building, Aadesh came out and stopped him.

"Jay hold on, hold on!"

"What?"

"I'll get you to Philadelphia in six hours, but you have to tell me what is going on, and I am asking politely and nicely. I am not pushing you or ordering you. But I need to know, I am your only key right now for United States."

Jay peaked into his eyes, and then, broke his silence knowing he could trust him just a bit.

"Planet Nibiru exists, and it's arriving sooner than we think."

Jay and Aadesh had a silent moment together.

Over the dark quiet ocean went a jet at the speed of sound crossing the Atlantic Ocean. In the back was Jay with a helmet and oxygen mask in an F-14.

NSC- Houston, Texas

Ronald Williamson stood arrogantly tall and firm in the empty conference room with faded windows. Alex Jacobs stared at him without a concern on his face.

"What do you want me to say?" said Ronald.

"At this point it's not much about what you say but what you will do. I will not allow a problem like you to stand in my way." Alex clarified with Ronald in a business manner.

"I have no family, no kids, no relatives, nothing, roll your dice, and play the cards. I am sick and tired of your secrets."

"You're not leaving much room for discussion I see," Alex pointed out as he came around the conference room table.

"There is nothing to discuss Alex. We have aliens crawling up our ass, Russians and Iranians threatening every five seconds to disable our communication, White House jumping in our decision every 10 minutes, eating my head. I can't do this. If I can't put certain things to use, then I am not going to be wasting my time helping to build things that are just going to rot in the dust."

"Who do you think got the Internet, wireless cell phones, High Definition technology and GPS system out to the word in a matter of few years? It was me, and I will fix this when the time is right, but you need to keep your schizophrenic mouth shut and start taking your pills," said Alex.

"Oh nonsense, I was the one fighting and having meetings every single night for two years trying to convince your slow and selfish ass to get the technology back to the people who built them," Ronald replied. "It was me, not you, going to overnight meetings at the White house to have the GPS technology approved."

"The people didn't build it. We just copied our way with their technology; I mean imagine what the world would be without the 1946 Incident. As far as you referring to our scientists down below, my check book takes care of them," said Alex.

"I really wish there is a hell, because you belong in it," Ronald replied as he gave him a dead stare.

"So do you Ronald, so do you. I'll prepare your document for your departure tonight, but your memory will be getting sterilized in the next 15 minutes," said Alex as he opened his coat and showed Ronald a 9mm gun on his belt.

"You know I've been trained not to think when using this weapon, so please cooperate, and I know you will," said Alex.

Smoke covered the airway in a small conference room while Clark was sitting amongst 20 other people. On the table lay empty coffee cups, paper pads, laptops, chips, half eaten burgers, with cell phones and all the necessities needed to be staying up late.

"Alright settle down people," announces Clark to the chaotic room, where no one had a clue about how to solve this problem.

"Settle down!" He repeated himself again, loudly.

The loud noise of crowd became quiet as they all sat on their chairs.

Clark took some chalk and drew a circle on the board, and five X's around it. Then, he overrides the X's with a bigger X in a blur color over the whole drawing.

"We got 25 satellites, worth more than 56 billion dollars that are hovering like dead beats in the orbit. What the hell is going on?" asked Clark.

The entire scientific group bit their lips and looked at one another, but didn't have a single word to say.

Clark stood still as he glanced at each face.

"No cell phone, no email, no Internet, no faxes, and no hard line communication, forget talking to Tony Blair, I can't even order pizza from Pizza Hut. No television, no radio, no crack-jack," said Clark as he becomes more frustrated.

"What in Jesus' name is going on? It's complete nonsense," yelled Clark.

A man in the back raised his hand slightly and turned to his left to show his face.

"Have we looked at this as a possible terrorist threat?"

Clark glanced at him as he held his chin.

"They are looking into it, but even the terrorists need communication, so we don't think there is any possibility for that to be happening. But, as I said they are looking into it," replied Clark.

"This is the worst damn day in the history of our technological life, all you MIT useless brains can't do squat, Can't do squat!" Clark yelled.

"I am not a big man in my profession. I am only ordered to find answers and yell at you boys. So might as well give me something so I can tell them upstairs. There is a signal that came in 4 hours ago, a signal from outer space. Right now at this time all we can do is talk and discuss, and wait, so let's talk. What is this signal and what is its purpose?" asked Clark as he took a sip from his coffee.

All the top directors stood outside the door watching Clark helplessly seek answers. There was a sign of defeat in the age of science and technology for the entire scientific community.

From the very back, Larry Page stood up; a 32-year-old Italian male with a very convincing look.

"If this signal or aircraft might have landed on our planet, it certainly doesn't want us to document their existence or whereabouts, am I right? They know our technology is only based on radio and video waves, which is actually good, at this time I can care less for losing my employment with this company. But, I once heard that there is a secret vault. I am sure you've heard the stories and rumors yourself, but there is a vault where they are developing a laser signal. It will be just like your radio and video signal but only 1.2 million times stronger and accurate, not to mention undetectable."

Clark suddenly got up with a spark in his eyes.

"Hold on, you are actually implying that the rumors are true?" Clark asked.

"Actually I am not implying, it does exist. I just don't know where it is but all we have to do is reach into the vault with Ronald Williamson's approval and we could be in business. They think we may not be as advanced to go beyond the radio waves, that's why there is a good chance they might not have deactivated our laser technology," replied Larry.

Clark went up to Larry and landed a kiss on his forehead and hugged him. He then grabbed his coat and ran outside the conference room.

CHAPTER 10

TRUTH REVEALED

Clark came running towards the director and board members as they stood in a cluster. He stormed in their direction and pulled Williamson aside, and bluntly asked him about the rumor. "I need to get into the vault right now and test that laser signal," Clark halted and caught his breath. Now don't deny it, I know it exists, and I will do whatever it takes for you to reveal the truth," said Clark.

"What are you talking about?" asked Williamson.

"Williamson, don't you dare say a word, since this is our only chance, and you've got to do this without the White House's approval. Listen, we have less than two hours before they attack," said Clark.

Williamson pondered for a while, sighed and then started walking towards a white wall, "follow me," he told Clark.

Clark began following him heading towards the wall and asked, "Why are we going to a dead-end?"

Williamson kept walking as he approached the wall and glanced back at Clark. Some random people who were working and talking with other scientist stopped as well, and glanced towards the wall suspecting something.

Williamson took out a black five-inch tube and pressed a button. He then took three steps back and pressed another button on the device. A green laser beam appeared. He made a shape of a door on the wall with the laser.

At that moment the entire group of NSC employees had their undivided attention on the wall. Williamson took out a red device, poked it in the wall, and then twisted it 180 degree. The device contained green light, which turned on.

He again turned the device and pulled it back as the entire wall shaped door opened itself. Behind the door was a silver elevator.

"Step in," said Williamson to Clark, who was silent as he stepped inside the elevator and was unwilling to accept what he just witnessed.

Williamson punched some other button and the door closed back, while the wall returns back to its normalcy. The people outside were utterly confused and shocked. The quiet moment faded away for Clark, as he realized that the elevator was not only descending downward but also nearly one hundred and twenty stories down. He felt pathetic and useless after realizing he had never known such an incredible secret.

Clark kept trying to figure out in his head, why has this man revealed such top-secret entrance to him and everyone else?

"So, why did you do it?" asked Clark.

"Well, because I simply can't afford to lose yet another good man," replied Williamson.

"I'm not a genius, so if you want to save someone, save those who are actually worthy," replied Clark.

"You're not?" asked Williamson.

"Not as worthy as Jack Crawford, and Jay Michael Verma," replied Clark.

"Well, that's more the reason why I cannot afford to lose another man. Honestly speaking I'm simply ready for my vacation, because once I am dead; no one can come after my sins. Especially the ones I have committed in this temple."

"Jack is special, I know. I also know the construction place where he works now, and I am aware that he still continues to work on those equations he had been working on for the past seven years. But I have chosen to be silent about all this. Why you ask? Because I don't intend to allow his vision and his passion to become suppressed once again over budget related issues and pathetic top-secret agencies. I realize the answer we seek lay in his passion."

"Why can't you bring him back?" inquired Clark.

"That's not something that's up to me to do, it's their call. I got the notion myself, but once I realized what needed to be done, the big boys jumped-in and threatened to keep people like Jack, Mark, Jay and others out from the truth about this company. It is too much to accept for NSC that the scientist should be made aware of such information. Jack knows a lot about what went down in this place and if he chose to do so, he could've disclosed it to the public. However he realized that too much is at stake. Don't get me wrong, I even went all out in maintaining an eye on Jack. I couldn't have asked for any better protection for him. Believe me, she is good. In fact she was doing her job fairly well, up until she fell in love with him, which is why I relieved her of her responsibilities just a week ago."

"Who is she?" Clark asked.

"Laura. She is a bartender, who I paid every month for the last year and a half to keep an eye on Jack. But love is a strange thing; it can decode the codes for any bank account and heart. She sent back all the saved funds. Love seems to hold more importance than money."

"I see. So how long have you been working on this laser signal for?"

"About five years ago we found it near a crash site in Alaska. It must have been their curious young rebel who left the boundaries of his star system to enter ours, because there was only one alien body inside, which, too, was only nineteen years of age. Jack almost over heard me talking on my cell one night about the crash, and I knew right-there-&-then he must be discharged that very night. But the very next day his entertaining presentation about diamonds and Mayans took him out of the game without me pulling any stops. Believe me, if I had to do it again, I would actually involve Jack in that project. I know he's not making things up about planet Nibiru, Mayan, numerology, or what the heck you want to call it. We've already detected its magnetic field, but it's a dark, almost invisible planet that will approach the boundaries of our solar system in less than 10 years. Clark, every time I drop or cut someone from the department it contributed to my reasoning of leaving this place more and more."

"You're a decent man Williamson, but we all make mistakes. I know this place uses us like vegetables," said Clark.

"I know and I am just one of many who turned this place into a corporation as opposed to a scientific society."

The elevator had about sixty more floors to descend, as the flashing lights were visible through the thin opening from the middle of the doors. Clark felt a bit scared, as he had no idea what to expect down there. The horrific sound of dropping elevator didn't comfort him either.

"These scientists whom you are about to meet may be a bit strange, perhaps like myself, lost but conscious. They are not even aware of the 9/11 attacks, and I don't want this ignorance to prolong any further. These scientists aren't here by choice but are forced into this helpless situation. Their smiling faces hide the underlying issue that's been brooding deep inside. Your average American may feel that the Middle East is filled with a bunch of medieval people who need to be civilized. You know Clark, Islam happens to mean peace, hence it's supposed to be a religion of peace and yet what is delineated by the media, television, bureaucrats, governments, who distort us from the real truth. And why, might you ask? It's mainly for greed, corruption, power, oil, territory and control. Suppose if there was no oil in the Middle East; do you know it would've been a luxurious resort for the world? As long as we continue on this futile quest, our government will never allow peace to be present on this planet. The only man I came across who was the most honest politician after Kennedy; is Hugo Chavez, president of Venezuela. But, politics is a zero-sum game, and we did our best to make sure he didn't come in power and actually used the profit from the oil export to enrich his people."

Clark suddenly became curious and somewhat frightened as the elevator came to a complete halt. Williamson punched in a few more codes, as the elevator door opened-wide, while he placed his thumb on a small screen, which conducted a fingerprint identification.

The second glass door opened while a lady was found sitting behind a black desk. Williamson walked up to her, as Clark gradually followed behind him and scanned the entire area.

"Will you please identify this man with his proper authorization to be able to enter inside the lab?"

"I have it right over here," said Williamson while taking out a semi-automatic pistol as he shot the girl right in the head. She fell flat on the desk but no blood came out.

"Don't worry, she's a robot," Williamson went behind the desk and turned the body around. He reached to the back of her head and opened a small socket. There, he took out the CPU and put it in his pocket.

"Jesus Christ, she wasn't real? What the hell is happening on this planet?" said Clark.

"What about voice tracking and video surveillance in this place?" asked Clark, who was a bit shaken up from the shooting and discovery of the basement. He couldn't believe the scientist had created robots so real looking. Robots such as this had previously been merely an imagination of quality novels and Spielberg movies.

"I deactivated before we started descending down."

Both Clark and Ronald Williamson walked down the hallway, which was fairly empty with some light-gray walls and a bright shining floor.

"How many of these secrets are out there?"

While they walked steadily towards an enormous silver door Clark tried to ask questions to clear things up in his mind.

"Too many to count I suppose, but my first encounter with them was at the Roswell incident," said Williamson.

"You mean you actually saw them?"

"Oh yeah, I saw them," replied Williamson.

Clark waited for him to go on with descriptions of the aliens. However, when Williamson didn't answer; Clark again raised the question.

"What did they look like?"

"Well, you've seen the pictures on television and magazines haven't you?"

"Yes, I have," replied Clark.

"Actually they look nothing like that. Those four aliens looked as such, that your eyes and mind wouldn't be able to handle. After seeing those video footages and pictures, I couldn't ever look at myself again in the mirror anymore."

"Why?" asked Clark curiously.

Williamson kept looking down while walking, "They were the most beautiful beings one could ever see in this Universe. One look at them and you'll never look at yourself in the mirror."

"Where are they held now?"

"They are kept right here?" replied Williamson.

"Holy crap, are you for real! You mean right here, right now?" Clark repeated himself when Williamson didn't answer back. He became curious like a child.

"Oh yes," said Williamson, "but we may not have enough time to give the tour of the entire facility today."

Over on the base level, Larry Page told everyone to be quiet and act normal as if nothing had happened. He requested to all the lower level scientists who witnessed the amazing spectacle.

Ronald Williamson removed the gun once again from his holster, changed a node on the barrel and pulled the trigger. No bullet came out, but there was a twisting sound that was heard. He then rotated the bullet holder 180 degrees to the left as a code screen popped out.

Williamson punched in a very long code which he perfectly recalled. After punching in the numbers a laser door shape appeared on the wall.

Hooking the gun up in the small square, he turned it counter clockwise. A small portion of the wall opened up as an eye scanner came out, but instead of scanning his eyes they went around to his ears and plunged in like suction cups.

Ronald turned the large knob and opened the door.

"What was that all about? I thought it was supposed to scan your eyes?" asked Clark in a curious manner.

"There are lots of things in this world that are not going to make sense, especially in this place. The device was actually scanning my brain tissue, because eyes can be changed and replaced but the brain cannot, at least for now."

A huge hall about the size of fifteen football fields was filled with the most uniquely designed spacecrafts. There were other unexplainable things laying around, while only ten to fifteen scientists were working on them in different sections.

"Holy crap, you must be kidding me, right?" said Clark while stepping inside the dorm.

"This facility was completed in 1979 for an amount of $76 billion dollars. After the Roswell crash, scientists found many devices and methods to advance in technology, cellular phone, internet, wireless communication, fax, video conferencing, chemical weapons, satellite and the numerous space ventures we've indulged in since the sixties."

Clark and Ronald stepped down on a plate, which was smoothly pulling downwards, like in Pascal's ship on SYIRUX-82. As they were descending down, Clark again popped one of many questions.

"What about the lunar landing?"

"It was real, but we just had to take down the president to make it happen. He was going to share our secrets with the Russians regarding what's really on the moon, and, the fact that he ordered us to tell the world truth about our contact with the aliens. I heard someone say a while back, "If Kennedy was alive; this world would be a different place."

"That means the rumors about the moon are true?" asked Clark.

"Yes. A glass tetrahedron structure pointed exactly at 19.5 degree on the horizon was found half a mile from the landing sight of Orion 11. The figure 19.5 has been a very common occurrence in the calculation of various entities in this Universe. We've already landed a team of men on Mars fourteen years ago to investigate the ancient city of Cydonia which is again at 19.5 degrees from its poles. We have a secret launch site in South Pole, away from people, especially media for all these research.

The mathematics and physics that has been taught to 90% of the students in the world is only the 75% of what mathematics and physics really is, because if the world had all the tools, this universe won't be such a secret place anymore. Every single structure in this solar system is based on a 19.5 degree concept. That one figure is indeed a gateway to the 4th dimension. The double hexagon that was found on the north pole of Saturn was just a shadow casted from an object of 4th dimension which you and I can not see with our mindset. Only our alien friends can. This building is more mysterious than the Universe itself Clark."

Wanting to continue the conversation, Clark shifted gears and paid attention to this entire uniquely built lab.

"Why is there only a hand full of scientists in this entire area?"

"One too many I say. The more you have the more trouble you can run into keeping this place as a top secret. But it doesn't matter now, does it? It simply takes one rotten fish to expose it all. Like myself."

"What are they working on right now?"

"Time travel, 60% complete."

"D-65," yelled Williamson as he approached the men.

A middle-aged scientist with long beard and long hair came running towards him with a smile.

"Sir, how is your day going? I am doing fabulous. I am ready to work on any task you have for me. So, what would you like me to do?" asked D-65.

"What the hell..." whispered Clark to himself, He saw the man speak in total robotic manner.

"I need to gain access to the C16 vault. Please activate the codes," Williamson ordered the scientist.

"Yes sir! Yes, I'll get to it right away!" replied D-65 as he ran back into a small room on the side.

"You've brainwashed these people, haven't you? Or are these also robots?" inquired Clark who was quite angry at this moment.

"They chose to lead this life in exchange for $10 million dollars for six years of work. I don't think anyone would complain for a few years of brainwash," replied Williamson. Clark stared at him with a confused look, while D-65 called Williamson on a speaker "come inside sir. It's ready."

"They are not robots; robots still don't have the brain capacity that we humans have. Let's go and get your signal up."

Clark glanced all around while making a 360 degrees turn, watching and observing everything with a detailed eye. He passed by the remaining scientists who seemed to ignore him and Williamson, as though they weren't even in the room.

"Their minds don't even register your presence until you call them by their respective coded name," said Williamson.

"I happen to have a Ph.D. but right now I feel like a used car salesman," said Clark while he deeply observed the facility.

"Don't worry, soon you'll feel like a shoe salesman."

Together they walked into a room. Inside was a long box shaped device. D-65 was working on a computer and after he fiddled with a couple of keys, a cover started to remove itself above the device. Underneath was a blue and purple glowing gel in the middle of a glass tube. On the sides were keying pads and two small monitors. The device looked like a nuclear reactor. Clark walked around it with his eyes-wide-open. He was also intimidated by this machine. His eyes kept vacillating back and forth between the device and Williamson.

"D-65, will you please explain to Mr. Clark what he's looking at?" commanded Williamson.

"Absolutely sir, it'll be my pleasure. We call this Sexton signal, which is created by the Z24 and Antapon material that was found in one of the alien spacecraft about ten years ago in Alaska. They were using something similar to create invisible laser signals which travels 107 times faster than the speed of light with more accuracy than you can fathom. This signal cannot be detected even by another intelligent life, because the Z24 is a protective untraceable shield with a uniquely coded sequence on every launch, which is only detectable by the party who controls it. Its coding automatically changes every 30 seconds. And detecting the first sequence of coding will take more than 45 minutes to an hour for anyone to figure out. Unless you're some superior being," said D-65 with a smirk laugh.

D-65 punched in codes on side of the screen. The liquid began to blend together with the other half. Within the glass there were two black bolts on each side, which suddenly lit up. From inside the room, appeared a thick glass tube that hooked onto the reactor.

"All I have to do is punch in another code and the world would become a digital laser dome," said D-65.

"Activate it,' said Williamson in a very authoritative manner.

"But sir, this is..."

"Are you talking back to me D-65?"

"No sir, no I am not sir. But I love my family, please don't do anything to them sir."

D-65 quickly punches in the numbers and after that the reactor charged up a small hole on the ceiling. A thin blue laser beam shot up through the opening towards the sky thousands of feet above them.

"Keep it this way for as long as you can," said Williamson to D-65.

"Yes sir, as you wish."

Ronald Williamson slowly walked over to him and placed his right hand on D-65's head as he started chanting a code.

"Down to diminish, down to synch, up and over comes upon a blue bird, which will hold you in your cage."

After reading this to the scientist, Williamson rubbed his eyes with his fingers and stepped back.

D-65 spoke with his eyes closed.

"What is it that you want me to do? As I shall do it at the cost of my own life," said D-65.

"Do not let anyone enter these doors until the green light gets turned on your wrist," said Williamson.

"I won't, you shall be safe sir, and all the responding channels will be running via satellite within 30 seconds," replied D-65.

"Why did you hypnotize him?" asked Clark, in a very disturbed fashion.

"It's necessary, because soon enough someone will be coming down to turn off the signal," said Williamson as he and Clark started walking out of the room.

Both of them walked past the other scientists who just continued working like robots.

A strange man stood amongst a group of people on the streets of Philadelphia in the middle of the night. Suddenly he felt something in his pocket, as he became aware of his cell phone ring-tone. He quickly picked up the phone, as others around him turned their heads. Within seconds of his phone ringing, other phones around him also became active. People began to yell and scream on the phone.

Across the world the television started to work, the entire phone and radio communication systems came back online. In the prime-time news rooms there was complete panic and mayhem. The producers were grabbing the announcers as they made coffee, while others were sitting in the restrooms. At one news station, the cameraman brought his equipment into the makeup room as the female announcer was getting ready. There was a state of complete disarray as the announcer panicked from the live camera. She stared at the lens in shock, then, stormed out of the room holding her hair while the producer followed behind her.

"Hey, where are you going? We need you on right now," yelled one of the producers.

As the dawn of a new day started, a black military helicopter landed at an unknown airport. Several soldiers ran towards the chopper as the door opened for the passenger side.

Jay in a hurry came out of the helicopter and ran towards the lobby with the rest of the soldiers. After getting inside he rushed straight towards the phone without even taking a single breath and dialed a number.

CHAPTER 11

THE OTHERS

Jack was walking along a rocky pathway, while trying to figure out the boundaries of this invisible object. Laura, John and the kids were separated from Jack, but they were also engaged in scanning and searching. John and Michael were also busy eating candies. Both were lost in their own playful world. John kept a good distance from the hill because of the kids.

Jack's cell phone rang as he quickly picked up.

"Hello," said Jack in a hesitant manner since it came from an unknown number. He listened to the person on the other side of the phone as he heard the loud voice. His suspicion quickly evaporated about the unknown call. He gladly said hello and took a surprise hit knowing it was Jay Michael Verma. They both began to chat back & forth, discussing everything that was transpiring. Once Jack found out about Michael's arrival in United States, he requested him to be at his side. Jay gladly agreed and wanted to make an arrangement to meet. It was his mission to do so in the first place. They continued talking but Jay had to end the call.

Jack slowly started to turn his head around towards the hill and looked at all the people in panic.

"You are kidding me, alright you stay where you are and I am coming," said Jay while quickly hanging up. He walked over to the military personal and requested a vehicle immediately.

One of the soldiers spoke out, "you can use our reserved civilian hummer."

"Let's go," said Jay.

Jack suddenly started yelling to all the people near him. "Everyone step back, or they will attack, step back or they will attack," he yelled. After Jack made the statement, an invisible force threw a young police officer. It seemed as though he were pointing his gun in the direction of the noise.

Jack rushed to his family as he picked up Lisa and held Laura's hand.

"What's going on? What's happening?" asked Laura while walking swiftly and keeping up with Jack's pace.

"I just spoke with Jay Michael Verma, that Indian scientist I used to work with at NSC. He just told me that it's definitely 'something else, instead of Nibiruans.' He also solved the Numerological equation I was working on. In fact there is a good chance they will attack in the next four hours," replied Jack.

"Hey people, move, will you," yelled Jack to the crowd in front, while he tried to get back to his house.

"What the hell is going on Jack?" said John.

"I need to know if they are going to attack or not."

The entire crowd began to move backward running away from the small hill. "What is going on dad?" asked Michael when they all entered the house. "The aliens will be attacking soon," said John in a jocular fashion. "Oh cool, will they have the light sabers with them too?" asked Michael.

"Oh, now they'd better, if they are going to come and meet my grandson, or else I'm going to send them back to their nebula," replied John.

In the meantime Jack opened the basement door and rushed downstairs while everyone followed.

He brought the computer back out into the open, while there were two red keys glowing. He noticed them and so did Laura. But he didn't jump to any conclusion about them. He waited and observed while also trying to pay attention to the chaos outside. Laura came from behind and pressed the two keys. She didn't care as to who was in charge of the matter. She just wanted to get to the conclusion of this video journal.

"Welcome!" said Pascal looking right into the camera as the other crew members of his ship stood behind him, lined up in one row. He then handed the video to a robot, to follow him around.

The Sun had set behind the mountains but some light in the sky was still visible. The astronauts were all geared for the take-off. In the background one could see two robotic vehicles moving around, scanning and testing rocks and other objects of the planet Earth.

Next to Pascal was an extremely small car, which can barely fit two people, as it hovered three feet above the ground.

Pascal put his thumb on a scanner as the two ski rods glowed with blue color, lifting the vehicle, ascending it thirty feet into the air. The robot that was holding the camera also rose up by his laser jet rocket and followed behind Pascal's car.

They traveled over the icy-surface of the Earth for about a minute or two where the female astronaut pointed out a certain location. "That's section 34."

Pascal took his vehicle to area-34 and landed. They both got-off from the vehicle as the robot landed with them. He took out his transparent map and brought it over to the surface where he saw small sparkling rocks on the ground.

"We got it! Call the team over," said Pascal.

The astronaut reached for her helmet and pressed a button.

"It's there, come on over," she said.

And before she could press the button to turn the communication off, four huge vehicles came hovering above.

Two long laser strings came out from both sides of the craft as it kept transforming itself into something much more detailed and complex. Soon thereafter it turned into a drilling machine. After completing the transformation they headed straight for the targeted area, as a thick laser beam shot from within and into the ground.

After about a minute of penetration the craft moved up and with its two-laser string attached at the bottom, pulled out a 10 X 18 diamond rock. All the astronauts flew back to the main ship and laid the rock in front of SYIRUX-82. As soon as the uncut Diamond was laid down, three robots came and cut, cleaned and shined it into a typically shaped diamond.

"Our ship was damaged by the extensive heat from penetrating planets, comets, and stars for the paste 757 light years. As you can witness our robotic engineers are fixing the tiles in the section that are 70% damaged."

The robots continued to take small pieces of diamonds and began repairing the bad sections.

A black box was being brought out from the ship held by the hands of a woman. Lava came out towards Pascal. She tried to walk faster than others, almost as if she was in a hurry. She stumbled on a small rock and tripped as the black box went out of her hands into mid-air. Before it hit the ground, the KYIRUX computer shut off by itself.

"What? What the hell..." said Jack as he smacked KYIRUX on the side, at which point a green bar appeared that showed 7% of battery life remaining.

"Damn," whispered Jack to himself.

While Jack sat in the dark with the rest of his family, a ray of sunlight started hitting his face. He looked up at the window and noticed the Sun was rising from behind the hill. Jack opened his basement door and stepped out. The crowd was still gathered outside the house. He looked back at his family with a concern, "stay here," as he went out wearing a leather bike jacket with red and white stripes on it. He read that the time was six o'clock on the grandfather clock next to the antique cabinet; Just some of the leftovers from Jack's cynical divorce with Tracy.

The crowd had increased compared to last night, while they continued staring at the hill with their jaws dropped. Jack also found himself gazing at the unusual sight.

On top of the hill, steam and smoke was noticeable in four different directions without any object being present. Most of the people around were scared to get any closer, yet they didn't mind staying close enough to have a display of this brewing excitement.

The morning was cloudy but there was no sign of rain, which set an ambiance that was fresh.

"Hey Jack," yelled Donald, one of Jack's neighbors.

"Hey, what's going on?" said Jack.

"Well, that's what I want to ask you. What's up with the smoking guns, any NSC secret project that you know about?" asked Donald.

"Nope, nothing that I know of," replied Jack as he suddenly saw a bolt of lightening hit one of the police cars. It seemed to emanate from an unknown invisible source on the hill top. Screams were heard from the huge crowd, especially the women who were standing right near the hill. The chaotic situation became even more frantic.

Laura came running out towards the door. "What was that?" she yelled, as Jack was looking at the hill.

"Get inside, just get inside, something is going on," yelled Jack.

There was a new terrorizing sound that was heard among the people as they gradually stepped back. The freeway was jammed and blocked as the military hummers and tanks were penetrating the city of brotherly love.

"Reaching section 55-644 north longitude in approximately zero to fifty-six, the signal is located on 35 Pierce Street. Satellite images show a sizable crowd in the alley, 10-4 copy," said a soldier inside a military hummer.

"Sir, the signal is coming from Jack Crawford's house," said a soldier.

"What? Repeat that again!" replied Jay.

"The undefined signal is coming from within Jack Crawford's house."

"What? You guys have to move faster, please," yelled Jay as the hummer started honking at the traffic in front and rushed through the freeway even faster as it drove on the emergency lane.

The steam sound on the hill suddenly stopped as it grabbed everyone's attention again. The loud, paranoid crowd became silent; while there was amenity accrue to only one aspect.

The faces of these people were adorned with a concerned look from this unexpected silence. Laura took a few steps ahead. Behind her John was holding the kids but he too was ducked down and peaking in the direction of the hill.

Some police officers came through the crowd as their eyes were focused towards the mysterious area. Following them were dozens of German shepherds on leashes. Around 25 cop cars were flashing their lights at the end of the street. The dogs seemed to be barking aggressively as they rushed towards the hill. The crowd opened up to let the cops and their dogs through.

However before they could reach the edge of the hill, the dogs suddenly stopped and started to moan as they began to move backward. The police got a little worried and confused from the dogs' reactions.

They kneeled down and put their paws in front of their eyes, something they never did before which surprised most people around them including the cops.

Jack assessed the situation that was building up and whispered, "They are hostile."

"What?" said Jefferson, his neighbor who stood right next to him "We have to move and I mean move quickly," said Jack.

Just after those words were uttered from Jack; a loud horn drew everyone's attention to the frightening bellow. The sound was loud enough to break the windows of the houses and the cars. Panic grew among these people as they tried to disperse, but were unable to do so because of the overcrowding.

"Go inside, please go inside," yelled Jack to his entire family as Laura rushed into the house along with John and the children.

"You need to come inside as well," shouted Laura back to Jack.

"Everyone, settle down and moved back slowly, back up, back up," yelled one of the cops who were trying to restore balance to this brewing situation.

"Go from the side, go from the side sir and please don't push," another cop yelled.

A red glass window right above Jack's house was still fully intact.

The horn blew once again, and the red glass shatters and lands by Jack's feet as a few pieces end up on the car windshield.

Jack ducked down on the ground as he brushed off the glass from his body. The screams of the people got louder and louder by the second, while Jack began to stand up.

"Honey lets go," yelled one of the men whose wife was trying to grab all the things from the porch.

Jack gathered himself together. He took a peek through the red glass in the direction of the hill. Suddenly he froze and came down to the level of the broken glass lay on the car windshield. His eyes opened wide in panic as he saw a uniquely shaped craft near the hill. The spacecraft was about seven stories tall and dark gray in color. There was a strange current around the craft, which kept flashing every second.

Jack's hand began to shake as he picked the piece of broken red glass from front of the windshield. He put the glass close to his eyes and saw the alien-ship with small square boxes descending down towards the ground.

"Oh my God, oh my God, they're coming!"

Jack started yelling to the crowd, "listen up everyone, you can see them through the red glass, do you hear me, you can actually see them through the red glass."

Several people around him picked up the red glass and tried to visualize what Jack saw.

"You can see them, holy cow you can actually see them! Run everyone and get the hell out of here, they're coming for us," yelled one man as he started to break from the crowd and ran the other way.

Jack curiously moved forward towards the alien ship. One could only see it for a split second as the crowd blocked the view of the ship and the creatures descending from within.

"Jack!" yelled Laura as people try getting into his house.

"Laura!" Jack shouted as he tried to run back into the house.

He pushed people and threw them over the patio as they tried to mob his house. Somehow Jack managed to shut the door and lock it. Once inside he gathered everyone in his family and took them to the basement.

A state of complete darkness engulfed the basement while screams and yelling of women and children could be heard outside.

"All right everyone, stay calm," said Jack in the darkness.

CHAPTER 12
THE GATHERING

Clark was on the cell phone listening to someone in a loud and paranoid voice. After fully hearing the other person out Clark replied, "You can see them through the red colored glass?" he whispers.

Clark stared at Williamson for a brief moment and then returned back to his conversation with the person over the phone.

"Jay, wait for me there; no matter what…don't leave that area. I'm leaving right now to come over, because I need to see this with my own eyes, do you hear me don't leave. I'll make it, one way or another, but I am coming."

"I know, I'm sending a helicopter down for you, tell them code 799093-LAKERS. And no one's going to ask you a single question after that," replied Jay.

"I'm on my way," replied Clark as he shut his cell phone and quietly walked over to his desk and grabbed his jacket and some paperwork.

He sneaked out of the boiler room. While walking he swiftly looked back at the door. He started running towards the parking lot and jumped into his car. Clark scanned the entire area to see if anyone was following him. He quickly started his car and raced off from the parking lot. Inside Ronald Williamson finally took his medication ZYPREXA as he felt dizzy and somewhat disoriented. Instead of the side effects, the medication actually gave him a sense of reality. He had a slight idea of what might had happened in the past several hours.

"Where is Clark? Have you seen him? Hey Tim, have you seen Clark?" asked Ronald as he came rushing inside the mainframe area.

"He was just here on the cell phone, about five minutes ago," replied Tim.

"I see…has anyone seen Clark?" yelled Williamson. Larry Page stayed quiet, and kept minding his own business.

"Yeah, I just saw him outside sir," yelled one of the security guards as he stood at the door.

"Where did he go?" inquired Ronald.

"Well, I just saw him take-off in his car from the parking lot," replied the security guard as he held the door for Williamson.

Ronald Williamson ran outside, as everyone started to wonder the reason behind him looking for Clark.

"He isn't going anywhere," whispered Williamson to himself.

"What car is he driving today?" asked Ronald in an aggressive way.

"Red corvette," replied the security guard.

"Get the pilot for the chopper on the pad. I am going to the roof."

"Get him up there, now," Williamson yelled to the security as he ran towards the elevator.

"Yes sir," said the security guard who took out his radio and called for a pilot.

"I need a pilot immediately for take-off on G-Line from building H for Ronald Williamson, copy-over," said the security guard.

"Fly bird XTX88 is now confirmed for Roland Williamson, 10-4," said a lady on the other line.

"Copy that," replied the security.

Clark rushed through the city streets, as he tried to get on the freeway. "Jay, did you meet up with Jack yet?" Clark inquired while on the cell phone.

Jay ran out of the hummer on to the street towards Jack's house, while trying to go against the flow of the citizens. The soldier kept watching Jay as he penetrated through the heavy crowd.

"I am on his street trying to get to his house. I can see it from here but there is no sign of him, he must be inside. There's a bunch of people standing in front of his door, it seems the crowd here is going crazy."

While rushing against them, Jay saw a piece of broken red glass that he picked up and put in front of his eyes.

A small group of citizens with small rocks in their hand tried to break the red glass window of a very classy and private African American male's house. The house owner stood in front of them in panic, but then, was forced to step-aside as the mob of people broke the living room and the upstairs window. The man had a British accent as he tried stopping the people.

Jay peeked through the glass, as his jaws dropped. Just in front of Jack's house a craft stood on a single leg of steel.

Jay ran even faster towards Jack's house.

Darkness still absorbed the basement, as a match sparkled in front of Laura's face. It found its destination as she lit the candle.

"What's going to happen now?" asked John.

"They're coming after us, I guess," replied Jack.

"What?" said Laura as she stared directly into Jack's eyes who looked a little confused.

"Don't you know that they are coming for the computer?" He replied.

"Dad you're scaring me," said Lisa as she held Jack's hands even tighter.

"We cannot stay here longer," said John, who could clearly hear the yelling and screaming of other kids on the street.

"And we can't be outside either," replied Jack.

"Then what do we do?" said Laura.

"What do you mean by what do we do?" stated Jack.

"I mean, are you going to risk our lives for the computer?" asked Laura in frustration.

Jack stared at her without blinking his eyes; meanwhile a loud knock was heard on the door. The knock occurred three times and then, there was brief silence.

Michael and Lisa started crying softly as Laura quickly picked Michael and Lisa up in her arms, while Jack stood up. Their attention was drawn back to the door where the knock was now heard six times. Then after another abrupt silence there were nine knocks on the door.

"Three, six, nine, it's a pattern," said John.

Jack tried to rush upstairs as Laura motioned to stop him without making any noise. He gently pushed her aside and reached the basement door to put his ear on it. Jack knocked on the door twelve times. He waited for a short while but there was no answer back. Then, after six more seconds there was a knock for fifteen times. After hearing the pattern Jack opened the door.

Jay Michael Verma stood outside the door. He rushed inside and closed it immediately.

"How did you make it here this fast?" asked Jack.

"I solved the equation which was missing the diametric pattern towards section 3.1 on the 42nd sector. I don't think it's them, but I am more confused than before."

They both rushed downstairs, but before they were on the last stair, another knock was heard on the door; however this was a much louder knock and occurred only once. A strange sound faded in from the outside, like that of someone talking or whispering.

"Let's go," said Jack, in a husky voice to Jay while showing him the computer.

"What is this?" asked Jay as he followed right behind Jack.

"First you tell me how the heck you got here so quickly? And how exactly were you able to find my address? And, How did you flyover without any communication?" asked Jack.

"Took an F-14 straight from India, if you got the cash under the table, they'll take you to the moon, and it's not too hard to find the address of a Ph.D. doctor living in the ghettos of Philadelphia," replied Jay.

Jack opened a small door in the corner of basement, which led to a small tunnel, perhaps something that was made by him, for these situations.

"Oh by the way guys this is Jay Michael Verma, one of my friends at NSC. He just came all the way from India in less than six hours. This is my dad John, my son and daughter Michael and Lisa and my wife Laura."

Laura was out of words by the way she was introduced, and couldn't help but smile softly in this time of panic.

"Hey how are you?" said Jay as Jack got his attention back. They all began to merge inside this small opening; however, when it was John's turn, he got caught in the hole because of his size.

"Damn," said Jack as he tried pushing his father through the hole by grabbing on his butt. He then used his entire back to get him through.

"Help me out here, will yaa?" Jack told Jay.

"Oh yeah, sure," replied Jay.

"Okay, who ever just touched me like that is a dead person unless it happens to be a gorgeous lady," said John as he was still stuck. "Hey…I am going to kick your ass," yelled angry John.

"So what's inside this thing that is so important to these aliens?" Jay inquired while pushing John inside.

"This is the answer to our entire existence, which happens to be a five hundred million year old computer that these aliens are after," said Jack.

"Well, I don't know about you pal, but I sure am not giving this to anybody, until I peek at it," said Jay.

"It's a theme park tour to the alien's world," replied Jack as he got inside the small room.

"Holy cow, we're actually being chased by aliens, I forgot about that for a second, man my kids would never believe me," said Jay as he paid attention to the creaking noise coming from up above.

Laura and the kids were the first ones to come out in the back of the house, as all the men followed.

"Laura, hold on!" warned Jack, as he took out a red glass from his pocket and scanned the entire back of the house and the rooftop.

"Go out the fence," instructed Jack to everyone.

They all ran crossing the fence and came out in a back alley. Jack quickly glanced back towards his house with the red glass, while a small craft landed in the front.

"Hurry, I think they saw us," said Jay.

All six of them headed swiftly through the back alley, while Jack held the computer. Laura led the way as she took a sudden left turn, while the rest followed her.

A helicopter took off into the air with Clark in the backseat, as he glanced at his watch. The chopper contained two other officers and a Pilot.

"How long will it take us to get there?" inquired Clark.

"I'll get you there in less than 1.5 hours sir," replied the pilot.

"How can you be sure?" asked Clark to the pilot.

"Ah, because it's a U.S Air-force aircraft sir, so I don't suppose you're going to get any better assurance than that!" replied the pilot.

"I'll take your word on that," replied Clark.

"You must be someone important to be able to get this kind of a ride," states one of the army commanders in the helicopter.

"Well come to think of it, yes I am. After all, I made it out of 3.1 million sperm cells, so that ought to be special," said Clark in a jocular tone, as the helicopter took off for Philadelphia.

Meanwhile Williamson was sitting inside yet another helicopter that was trying to build thrust.

"What the hell is the problem here, why don't you guys take-off already?" said Williamson to the pilot in frustration.

"I'm sorry sir, but I need to warm up the chopper before we can take-off," replied the pilot.

"God damn it, I swear all this technology is useless, I thought I passed the bill ten years ago for extreme choppers."

"Only the U.S Air-force has those choppers sir, but here we go," said the pilot as the chopper slowly lifted in the air.

Jack and the entire gang tried to hide in an empty, beaten down house. They all kept taking quick breaths while panting from running. John was laying on the ground with both his hands and legs all spread out, while he gasped for air.

"Son, next time you find a computer in the dirt, please, just leave it there," said John.

"Why is it that I want to agree with you on this one dad?" replied Jack.

"Okay, this is the situation, we need to increase the battery life of this computer," said Jack to everyone.

Jay started analyzing the computer and noticed one blue button lit on side of the computer.

Jack without any hesitation pressed the blue button, which caused two blue plates to come out, from each side.

In the middle of the computer's surface, a small screen popped up that showed a figure of a human hand. Jack quickly figured out what it was and placed both his hands on the plate. Jay curiously watched the entire exercise.

The two blue plates started to turn red as the computer battery power increased from 7% all the way to 50%.

Jack removed his hand and felt a little dizzy.

Jay glanced over to his hand and noticed two spots with blood on them in a circular shape.

"Oh wait, that thing is getting its energy from your blood?" Jay told Jack while carefully observing his palms.

"Now, why would it do that though? I guess blood does have a source of electrical energy in it, strange, but not," replied Jack.

"What the hell is this thing, and how do you turn it on? What's inside this machine man? come on tell me," said Jay, in a very anxious tone.

Sweat kept pouring down the corner of Jack's face as he grabbed the computer and placed it in front of him.

"Let me show you," said Jack, as he pressed the KYIRUX logo on the computer.

The white screen appeared and a robot came in front of the screen and explained the meaning of the word "KYIRUX."

"KYIRUX, meaning power of information. It also stands for God of Information," said the robot and walked away.

The screen faded out while another one appeared with Pascal sitting in a dimly lit room that had a gray and white theme in the backdrop.

"Are they here? Have they got to you?" asked Pascal in a very dramatically panicked mode.

"Our ship is dying and we need to repair it much quicker than we are able to. An ice storm is headed our way and my scientists are working on changing its direction but several components of our ship are malfunctioning due a mysterious compound that we haven't encountered anywhere in this Universe. We've been able to control weather, climate, and seasons for the last 2.1 million years on our planet. If we are unable to fix these problems, we cannot get to the White Gates."

Pascal stood up and started talking as the robot followed him with a pen. He got into the narrow hallway of his ship and moved forward, taking a right turn, which led to the exit, where nearly 77 astronauts were running around in disarray and talking amongst themselves, trying to fix SYIRUX-82.

Lava came running to Pascal from the darkness.

"Captain, captain that was our last package, the rest is all frozen," said Lava.

"Then, it must be this planet's fate, it's not in our hands anymore," replied Pascal.

"I'm sorry, for picking up the wrong package and breaking it," spoke Lava emotionally.

"It wasn't up to you, it is the decision of the Universe, but this place isn't so bad either, I suppose…" stated Pascal.

Suddenly Jack heard someone coming from the front door as only their shadows were visible. He quickly shut the computer down by pressing on the KYIRUX button.

Everyone's attention went towards the creaking sound of footsteps coming near the house.

Lisa and Michael hid their face underneath Laura's jacket.

Jay slowly crawled to the edge of the rack and glanced down. The shadow was not that of a normal human being, as it was unusually slim and tall in height.

"They are here!"

Jack tried to figure out a plan of escape. His eyes scanned the room. On the roof top there was a small opening as sunlight peeped through. He then looked around and spotted a wooden log and picked it up. After carefully calculating their estimated time of entry into the house he threw the log outside from the opening, as it landed pretty far off in the backyard.

Immediately the figures started tracing the sound of the log thinking that the humans they were pursuing had jumped off the rooftop. Meanwhile, Jack picked up Michael with the computer and Jay picked up Lisa. They all stepped down from the ladder and quietly started to run outside.

Stepping out the front, all six escapees began running to the other side of the alley. Jack passed on a red glass to Jay.

"Take a look at it and let me know if you see anything," said Jack while running.

Jay looked through it while running, "The small spaceship is moving forward. No wait, it's turning around and heading in our direction now."

"Just keep running and keep up man," said Jack as Jay fell a little behind.

He realized his slower pace and sped up. John kept lagging behind at which point Jay utters, "It's your dad, and not me who has to keep up."

"Hurry up dad," said Jack.

"Forget this, let them just take me. It'll spare the rest of us from working up a sweat," said John.

"Shut up dad, just keep running, you can do it!" replied Jack as he turned around to help his father.

"Here, go right," said Laura as she found an open door in the empty house.

" Are you sure?" asked Jack.

"Yes, it's safe let's go," said Laura.

"Hurry, they are gaining on us," said Jay as they all run into the back of the house.

While they are running inside, Jack noticed something.

"This place looks very familiar," said Jack while he ran inside with Michael in his arms.

"We're back to that same house," said Jay.

"God, you're kidding me," whispers Laura.

Far away in distance another sound was heard.

"Go back upstairs," said Jack.

"No wait, there is a basement," said John as he spotted a small door underneath the staircase.

It was fairly dark and creepy in the basement as any person could easily hide in the junk that was lying around. Heavy spider webs decently occupied the basement. The stairway was broken and was squeaky as a result. They came downstairs and headed straight towards the back.

First thing Jack did was to re-open the computer. The footage commenced from exactly where they left off previously. Pascal stood right in front of the ship as he spoke into the camera.

"I don't believe your technology is advanced enough at this time, but it will come up to the standards of this Universe as I will provide you the helpful blueprints to our advanced civilization and technology."

A woman came up to Pascal and handed him an electronic device.

"I am going to faint," said Jay somewhat excitedly.

"Shh!" motioned Jack.

Pascal opened a tablet computer with an electronic pen and started writing things on the screen.

"This right here is something like an encyclopedia of the Universe and all the things you'll need for survival outside your planet."

"I'm going to place this entire book into this small device."

Pascal showed a very small black chip that was about an inch wide.

"This device will hold up to 20.1 billion terabyte of information in it. I realize it's not a very large number, however, it's enough for this information to be fully placed inside."

He put the small device inside the notebook and punched a code with his pen.

Tear dropped from Jay's eyes as he moved back and placed his hand on his mouth from shock.

"You're crying now, wait until you take the complete ride," said John who was sitting on the side with Laura and the kids.

"Now that the aliens have landed on your planet you must protect yourself from them if they are hostile," said Pascal as he sat down on a rock.

"If you feel that your life is in danger, it probably is because down at the bottom there is a small symbol of KYIRUX which is a traceable chip that gives these aliens your whereabouts, from city to city, house to house, and their galaxy to your galaxy. It functions as a GPS navigation system."

Jack quickly turned the computer around and noticed a small KYIRUX logo. He held it and tried to twist it, but nothing happened; then he shifted the logo vertically and the small chip slid right out from underneath the computer.

He grabbed the tracker and ran towards the small window in the basement. Jack got up on a broken stool and broke the chip into two pieces and threw it outside into the backyard.

Jack returned back to his family as Jay was holding the computer in his hand. He pressed a button out of curiosity, as Pascal reappeared on the computer screen and said, "Mera naam Pascal hain," He spoke in Hindi language introducing himself to Jay.

"He speaks Hindi?" said Jay from his utter curiosity.

"I don't think so, that's weird," replied Jack.

"No it's not. The computer identifies your fingerprints and its origin. It then, translates the information inside; best suited for you to understand," replied Laura.

"Oh right, the Jewish thing," said Jack.

"Nice, she just kicked your ass Jack," said John while relaxing against the wall.

Across America an unexpected tension was rising since Philadelphia was under attack by the alien race. Every man and woman was glued to the tube at home, as they were unable to go anywhere since businesses, malls, groceries and various other places were closed in this time of chaos.

The streets of Philadelphia were packed with people resembling the sight of the "Million Men March." Almost thirty military helicopters were hovering over the crowded area.

The helicopters in the air had red glass hooked in the front of each main window to visualize the alien target.

Simultaneously, the alien spacecrafts seemed to be mobilizing themselves in the direction of the helicopters containing the red glass. A finger came out and punches several buttons. A red ore around the ship turns green which suddenly makes the red glass technique obsolete and pointless.

"Wait a second, the ship just disappeared," said one of the pilots in the helicopter.

"What do you mean disappeared? Keep looking through the red glass," replied the commander in the control room.

"No, it just vanished and I can no longer see it through the red glass, copy over," said the pilot.

"Get the Secretary of State on the line, fast," said the commander, as he waited on the other line.

"Well, get him out of the shower."

The commander waited on the phone as the person on the other line got ahold of the Secretary of State.

"Open your damn television and then tell me if this isn't some urgent matter you dumb ass," yelled the arrogant and rude commander.

Clark ran out of the helicopter as two air force officers were escorting him.

"I need a vehicle right now!" said Clark.

"The condition here is really bad, the traffic hasn't even moved an inch in nearly eight hours." replied the pilot.

"Then whose crap am I here to clean up, if I can't even get into that area? Why wasn't I told before? I have to get there somehow," said Clark.

"We can make you airborne again and get you fairly near that area, but we won't be able to stay for search & rescue. Once you're on the ground, God help you."

"Fine, just get me there," replied Clark, as he ran back inside the helicopter, which took-off no sooner than he closed the door.

Jack's face was filled with grease and dust, a face he knew of every evening after his construction work. His blue eyes shined brightly in the darkness while the soft sunlight hit the back wall. In the back, Laura, the kids and John were laying down taking a nap.

Jay still kept looking at the computer in curiosity while also keeping a close eye on the window.

Jack's concentration was being divided between KYIRUX and the creatures, which were vandalizing the quiet ambience. Noises could be heard of the creature jumping off the roof and onto the backyard as it moved further and further away from the premises.

Jack, after observing closely returned back to the computer and turned it on again.

The screen adjusted to the shape and condition of the basement. On the screen it showed a clear image of two moons during night time as Pascal stood right in front of the open sky.

"These are two moons of your planet which clearly have signs of oxygen below its icy water, but, it won't last for too long as these two bodies will be colliding with each other in less than three hundred and fifty million years from now due to an orbital imbalance. But there is a possibility that a new satellite might appear from the collision. I cannot guarantee if it will have life, oxygen or liquid water after the impact."

"We also have calculated the satellite of the seventh body will also contain a vast majority of marine life under its icy surface in approximately three hundred million years from now. It belongs to the biggest planetary body in this star system. This particular planet was supposed to be a mini star with sixteen planets, but due its slow moving core, it cooled down and turned into a gas giant. Three of its twenty one satellites will collide with the planet due to its strong magnetic pull. This event will happen in 12.5 million years from now."

Jack glanced at the keyboard as two keys were glowing bright green. He pressed them together as a small opening appeared from the top of the computer and a black device popped out.

"You might be thinking that you do not have the proper device to transfer the data, especially with the technology that is available to you, but you need not worry. At this moment your computer will be able to convert any binary data into a workable device. Hence if you look below there are pins coming out from the chip, you'll notice they are easily applicable to your technology to transmit information." The socket was of USB connection, which was easily recognized by Jack.

Jack put the device in his pocket. Jay at this time was speechless from the entire event.

Pascal started to put on apparel which resembled a thick white jacket and began to tie the belt around his waist.

"As I now leave your planet, I will surely hope that you forgive me for the mistake my junior scientist had made earlier, that has halted your original formation which could had taken place on this planet. However, at the same time I believe all this has given a boost in the grand scheme of things."

"What the hell is he talking about?" asked Jack.

"Your morning star will rise in about two hours which will give us lift off through solar and magnetic energy. Even having such advanced technology we are still uncertain about our mission. As I was previously saying, your planet currently has a very strange gas in its air that we have not encountered in our lifetime. This is why we are unable to figure out some malfunctions on our ship. " Pascal paused for a moment, but then continues with his speech.

"We are you, and you are us, or perhaps this is a natural mutation process, where one life gives birth to another. Our first law of being space travelers is not to leave a trace of our existence and just to let the Universe do its part. However, this time we are leaving something behind for this planet to help itself evolve."

The computer again showed a low battery warning at 10% of power remaining. Jack noticed the energy drainage.

"Damn, okay, where is the plate? come out, come on out!" said Jack anxiously as he waited for the plates to suck his blood.

A heavy thump occurred on the rooftop as Lisa and Michael were awakened from their sleep.

"Where are we?" said Michael. But before he could finish his sentence Laura closed his mouth and Lisa, too, as she was about say something herself.

The noises of footsteps were easily traceable above the basement.

Everyone looked towards the roof and listened closely, however, the noise suddenly stopped, and then, for a long while nothing was heard.

Everyone slowly brought their eyes to a level and only then, the noise picked up again. This time it was right outside the basement door. All six of them gathered together while taking in deep trembling breaths.

The basement door started making a creaking noise as it began to slowly open. Someone started to climb down the stairs.

Jack's eyes opened wide from the graveness of the matter. The noise was heard on top of the basement as it slowly crept up behind Jay, Jack and his entire family.

Laura quickly picked up metal rods and handed one to John while keeping one to herself. Meanwhile Jack tried peeking from a section to see who was coming down.

He scanned the area and suddenly opened his mouth wide and stood up.

"Jack," whispered John, as he warned Jack, before any foolish move was made his son.

"Clark…!" said Jack as Clark trembled from the shock and fell on the trash can.

"What is this? Some sort of a NSC reunion, who sent out the invitations?" said Jack as he helped Clark up.

"Jay," said Clark as he stood up and balanced himself.

"I gave him the address for your house actually. I think he might have something for you," said Jay.

Jack hugged Clark saying, "This is unbelievable."

"I am simply happy to see you alive and covered in mud," said Clark while he laughed.

"We don't have much time though, we need to get out of here," said Clark.

"Why, what's happening?" asked John from the back.

"John, Michael, Lisa! Oh goodness, your entire family is here? Thank God!"

"So, when did you get married?" asked Clark even though he knew who Laura was. He gave her the look that could easily be understood by anyone. But Clark knew he didn't want to bring anything up from what Williamson discussed with him. He kept his silence and acted like he was just being introduced to her.

"Today, well I was going to anyway. Oh by the way this is Laura," replied Jack.

"You definitely got the right guest list for the occasion," said Clark.

He also noticed the computer in Jack's hand "What is that?"

"I'll tell you all about it, but first we need to get out of here."

Williamson flew through the city. He instructed the pilot to go over Clark's residential area.

"What is the mission for sir?" The pilot asked.

"It is a matter of National Security. It's a must that I catch him," replied Williamson.

"Why is that sir?" asked the pilot.

"I'm only just realizing a mistake that I made a few hours ago."

"Delta two, Delta two, come in, over!" a voice spoke over the microphone.

"Yes, this is Delta two over sector 85, come in over," said the pilot in the chopper.

"We just received the confirmation that Clark Gabriel was dispatched in a C-26 chopper about an hour ago to Philadelphia, he's already on ground there, over," said the voice again.

"God damn it!" said Williamson in anger as he threw off his headphone. "What do you want me to do at this time sir?" asked the pilot.

"Go back," said Williamson in a depressed and lifeless manner.

A cell phone in Williamson pocket rang as he struggled to take it out and no sooner than he took the phone out from his pocket, he saw the number, and by that number, his demeanor changed.

"Yeah," answered Williamson.

"I think we need to have an urgent meeting with you. It's the President's order," said Alex on the other line.

"I got you," said Ronald Williamson and hung up the phone.

Ronald looked out the window and saw the trees and the water down below and spoke to himself, "I'm going to miss this place."

His hand reached up to his collar, as he searched for a capsule type locket hanging around his neck. He pulled the locket and opened it up. Inside it was a cyanide pill. He stared at it for quite some time and then, popped the pill into his mouth.

The chopper cleared the air as it landed once again at NSC's headquarters.

In the back Ronald Williamson was found sitting in his seat completely still, as though he was in deep sleep, while the chopper still kept roaring. The pilot shook him but Williamson stood still. After checking his carotid artery the confused pilot called for help.

CHAPTER 13

POINT BLANK

The bottom tip of the Sun was touching the mountains as twilight evening was gazing the skies of a fresh Earth.

Clark, Jack, Jay, John, Laura and the kids were going through a forestry area, which was an uphill walk. Jay was holding Michael and Clark was carrying Lisa. Reaching the top seemed to be a struggle for John. Everyone's clothing was full of dirt, including their faces.

Clark moved a little quicker and went up to one of the orange trees. He reached up and ripped off an orange for Lisa.

Jay followed in his steps and started grabbing the oranges. He threw them off to Jack, John and Laura.

John opened the orange up in a hurry, and in no time John ate the whole orange. Next to him Jack was doing the same while looking at his dad.

Everyone started eating, as they sat on the dried mud of the forest. While eating, Clark started laughing for no apparent reason.

Jack, too, laughed with him but questioned him at the same time. "What's wrong with you?" said Jack.

"Last night I couldn't have even thought of being here, eating an orange in the middle of the forest..."

"Life doesn't surprise me anymore," Jack replied.

"I think so too," said Jay who took a comfortable position and lay down while eating up the orange. "I mean what were the chances of three long lost best friends coming together; especially under these infinitesimal circumstances and in such a complicated situation."

"Look. The one mistake we made was to not look at it as a business and corporation, but that's one mistake I'm glad we didn't make," replied Jack as he finished his orange.

"I need to tell you guys something, I don't know if it's any bigger than our Mr. Pascal but it's big," said Clark.

"What is it?" asked Jay.

"I saw the secret chamber at NSC, which only you and I thought was some rumor. I saw it all, and I don't even have to describe to you who was working in there because you all must be wondering how the signal came back all over the world. It's not your normal radio waves, it's a laser signal which was experimented for the first time about 6 hours ago from the basement of NSC," said Clark.

"Tell me everything," said Jack.

<u>NSC BASEMENT-HUSTON, TEXAS</u>

D-65 stood calmly at the door, while in front of him were about seven huge guards dressed in black suites; as each one of them was about six foot three inches tall.

"I cannot let you enter this domain. My code has been locked, and I am not to follow any other commands. I shall protect this signal with my life," said D-65.

One of the men came up to him and threw a punch on his face, but D-65 held himself like a rock. The guard struggled and couldn't believe the strength this 5 foot 7 inch skinny man possessed. He didn't even move an inch after being hit. The guard hit him again, but D-65 held his fist and pushed it back in one motion and broke it in three different sections.

"Just kill him, his services are over," said Alex, head of the operation.

"What about the insurance? How should we cover that?" asked the guard.

"His age is around 45, I think a heart attack would be suitable now," replied Alex.

The guard took out a jet black gun and pressed a button; an electric current jolted out in a stream of wave and hit D-65 in his heart for about two seconds. Suddenly D-65 fell flat on the ground.

The men went inside, as another scientist in a white coat followed them. He went up to the computer and tried to shut it down. After punching in some codes he looked at a certain point in the room.

"He locked the code, it's impossible to decode it," said the scientist in a confused manner.

"What the hell do you mean impossible? Shut it down now," ordered Alex.

"He used the Matrix coding, which only he and Ronald Williamson were capable of decoding. The only way to shut it down is to break the device," replied the scientist.

"You mean to tell me that your incredible brain is useless against this code?"

"Give me some time sir, I'll do my best."

"You are not required to do your best; that is what I expect of you each time."

"Shut it down now," Alex yelled while walking away.

Night had fallen over the forest as Jack and Clark made a campfire out of wooden logs. Jay was bringing in the wood and settling it on the rest of the pile. The computer sat on the side quietly beside Laura, who was comforting the children.

In the middle of the fire a dead wild bore hung upside down.

"Oh man, the more I look at it, the hungrier I get," said John.

"I know, me too," said Laura.

"I want to say something to everyone here," said Jack.

"Speak captain," replied Jay.

"I want to tell you guys that it is because of this woman that I am alive right now, and because of this woman I am fighting this battle with a smile. Laura Dianberg; I love you with all my heart," said Jack while he stood next to the fire.

"I would say the same if you didn't look so scary under the fire, with all that mud on your face," Laura replied with a smile.

"Now, what did you see in this guy anyway? He's just a good looking Ph.D. scientist from NSC who pretty much solved the most important puzzle in the Universe," said Jay, who was turning the roasted pig hooked on wooden made rotisserie.

"I know, but I overlooked all that and saw that he was a good father and a good man. I think that was the only good thing about him that truly attracted me to him."

"Hey the Pig's starting to burn now, let's bring it down," said John as he got up and walked over to the roasting hog.

Clark and Jay brought down the cooked pig and laid it down on a huge pile of leaves.

Clark got out a pocket knife and started cutting the meat.

Jack waited and watched as they heard bubbles inside the stomach of John. "What? I haven't eaten in two hours," said John.

"Do you realize that for the past six hours none of the aliens have followed us?" said Jay.

"You're right, and for some reason I didn't even think we were being chased by them, where could they be?" said John, while a view of him talking to everyone could be seen from the interior of an alien ship hovering 40 feet above.

The monitoring of aliens zoomed on the KYIRUX computer.

The creatures conversed amongst themselves in their native language, while down on the ground John, Clark and Jack started picking on the pig's meat.

Jack actually started cutting the pig up with a sharp wooden stick. Laura on the other hand was feeding the kids first.

They ate and satisfied their needs. While John was a little bit more expressive than the others as he loudly burped towards the fire.

Jay, whose back was against the fire, felt John's wretched burp on his buttocks. "Jay your ass is on fire!" yelled Laura as Jay quickly sat on the mud and rubbed his butt.

"Sorry," apologized John.

Jack glanced over to the computer. He put the half finished bone down and walked towards it and held it in his hands.

He slowly brought it in front of him.

Clark and Jay, too, stopped, as they saw Jack zoned out on the computer. The whole forest was quiet as only the sound of burning wood was present.

"I know this thing has more than just a video to it, it has a lot more, a lot more to share," said Jack.

"What do you think it could hold?" Clark said.

"Let's finish up Pascal's journal in the meantime," said Laura as Jack glanced at her.

"I need to find out what happens to that box that went flying into the air. Remember, when the computer was shut-off while that box was in midair," said Jack while looking over to Laura.

"How do we go back though?" said John.

Jack pressed the KYIRUX button again as it turned its functions on. The invisible aliens above them gathered on the window, looking over to Jack working on the device.

"I remember the last time I pressed those two buttons for the video to appear."

"Press it again," said John as Jack pressed, and a white flash surrounded most of the area around them. Clark and Jay came running behind Jack.

"Oh my Jesus Christ," said Clark.

"Don't be so sure about him either," Jack spoke back to Clark.

"What the hell do you mean?" Clark asked.

"In their alien world, I saw a female getting pregnant by a beam of light, beam of light!" Jack said as he glanced back at the computer.

"Okay, now there must be something to go back, I don't think Pascal was finished, where do I..." as soon as Jack said it one key started blinking again.

The screen surrounded Jack, Jay and Clark with a pure white wall, as Pascal stood with his whole crew in front of SYIRUX-82.

"Welcome to the end of the journey, for you and I. I hope my conversation with you was helpful and a delightful event, the device you have in your hand is the fastest information-processing device in your entire galaxy. It runs on 5.5 Trillion gigahertz processor with 88.5 Trillion DPI Rational memory. Pretty much it's a human brain without any legs or arms. This device can do a lot more than just hold video synchronized clips of some alien like myself. If you look harder and with persistence you will find a guide and a map of this and other galaxies and everything we have found you shall know sooner or later. This is an indestructible device, which would need more than 18 million ton of Nuclear power to destroy.

"I wish there was more time for me to speak to you, but I do want to say one more thing. Your solar system is one of three star systems out of fifty thousand we explored, that has one planet going around your star, but not in spiral axis like this body and 11 other planets; but in elliptical axis and it does take about 600 thousand years for this planet to come back to the position where the rest of the planets exist. We also think that this planet may be able to sustain and grow life much quicker than your planet. I did want to imbed a log of this planet on the KYIRUX computer you hold, but there may not be enough time left, but this planet, which we have named Nibrathi, is capable of sustaining and growing life much faster than this planet," said Pascal as bright spotlights shined on top of Jack from the sky. All of them ducked and covered their eyes.

The horn of the craft whistled again.

"Damn," said Clark.

Jack grabbed the computer as everyone got up and began scanning the sky.

Clark and Jay carried the kids while Laura woke John up. They all started running towards the hilltop.

"We're dead, we're so dead," said Jay while running.

The spotlight started to follow them.

"I love you Jack, did I ever tell you that," said Clark while running right behind him.

"Whatever happens now, I know I am with the man I love and respect," said Clark again.

"Hey! What about me? Don't you love me?" Jay yelled while running up hill, and grasping for breath.

"I love you too. I have to say my life is complete now that I know the answer that we are not alone in the Universe," Clark replied.

"We are going to die right now? I wanted to finish more of that Ham, I only had two pieces of ribs," said John while trying his best to run behind them all.

"Dad, dad!" yelled Michael, who was terrified from all the commotion and running.

"Why are these people hunting us?" Lisa asked as she cried on Clark's shoulder.

"They are not hunting us, we are playing a game, they just can't catch us. If they do, then we lose," Clark replied.

"Are we winning or losing?" Lisa asked.

"Right now we're winning. We just can't have them catch us you know," replied Clark.

"Come on Mr. John hurry up," said Laura as she helped John run.

They were almost to the hilltop, but the spacecraft was getting lower and lower to the ground as they were entering a clearing devoid of any trees to hide under.

On the street of Jack's residence the people could see the full-blown spacecraft as it shined like a diamond in the sky at the edge of the hill. Several choppers went right after the spacecraft with full speed.

When the armed choppers reached a certain distance they got stuck and were unable to go any further in the direction of spaceship. All of them kept hovering in midair.

The rest of the 5 choppers experienced the same thing.

"Hold your fire, do not attack unless attacked upon," a voice spoke on microphone of the pilot's helmet.

"Copy over," said a very intense looking pilot as his helicopter was shaking while hovering in one spot.

"Seems like they have some sort of protective shield around it copy over," described another pilot who was trying to get around the ship.

The jellyfish shaped craft got closer to the ground.

Jack, with the rest of his famil, packed in tightly as the alien ship landed about 50 yards away from them. They had nowhere to run as everyone had reached the edge of the hill.

Jack put the computer down to the ground and held his two children while kissing them on their heads.

John also put his arms around Laura and Jack as his eyes released tears that were unstoppable.

The ship landed above the small hill. Within thirty seconds of landing all the lights went out as only dim yellow lights remained on.

There was a sudden stillness and quietness that overshadowed the darkness of the night. All seven of them watched in horror. Every second seemed like an hour, as they had no idea what was about to happen to them.

The silence from the ship and the ambience around it had an omnipotent feeling.

As they watch without blinking an eye, the ship stayed still without any action occurring around its surroundings.

"What is going on?" whispered Laura to Jack.

"I am just as clueless as you are, but whatever happens, I pray to God that I have you in the next thousand lives," replied Jack.

"I am scared," said Laura.

"Me too..." Jack whispered.

Then, in a split second the dim lights around the ship got bright in an instant and dimmed down again.

From the solid wall of the ship an outline of a door appeared in a pure white color. Once the door opened, a very tall, thin and blurred figure was standing behind it.

Jack slowly stood up with abundant curiosity towards this beautiful figure. The shape of this alien was sculpted in such a way where anyone can predict it was a female. The body was just like that of a human.

The figure stood at the door for a while and didn't move as they all watched with curiosity. The light from the interior of the ship shined softly on their faces.

The female figure started to walk down slowly and quietly.

Jack and the rest started to step back until they were pressed against a huge rock.

From the darkness came the most beautiful creature the human eye had ever seen. The figure was more beautiful than a normal female and gave a glow of peace and harmony. She was self glowing without any light from another source. Jack suddenly had a smile on his face as he felt calm and peace in his mind.

The alien smiled back, which showed she was not hostile. Inside the skull of the alien were little electric currents circulating all throught-out the body.

Jack fell to his knees, as if she were God. The rest of the family and friends also sat with him without moving their gaze from her.

"Hello Jack, my identity is ALIQA. I am an alien of the Planet VINNESTH, which is about ninety-seven light years away from your planet. I and my people don't come in any harm to you or your family. We are only here to learn what you have found for yourself. We are only here to learn about the ones who might have given birth to us. We received a signal that was far more advanced from your technology even though we have kept a close eye on your planet for a very long time, without ever touching it with our soul. But, we are in the same search as you and your people have been for many years, and we thought this might help us understand where we came from, and who might have created us. We can never harm you and your family Jack. That's not who we are."

Aliqa came close to Jack and put her beautiful finger on top of his forehead. Jack naturally felt a little awkward.

"I know every question and concern you have in life to this date; ask me anything you want, and I will answer it for you Jack. I know everything about you now."

"How did we get here? And are you Nibiruans?" asked Jack very nervously.

"No Jack, we're not Nibiruans, even we haven't been able to detect them or their planet, but we know it exists. It may turn out to be a greater discovery than KYIRUX, but for now, this is what we should celebrate," she replied.

"How did we evolve?" Jack asked.

"Do you trust me Jack?" asked Aliqa.

"Yes I do," Jack replied.

"I would need to hold that computer in my hand to answer that question for you," she replied.

"Please, I haven't even learned a single percent about this thing, please don't take it away," said Jack.

"We won't Jack, trust us," said Aliqa.

Hesitatingly Jack handed her the computer.

But instead of holding it in her hand she carried the computer in the air. Immediately, a male alien came out looking similar to Aliqa and took the computer by his gravitational pull. He took the computer back into the spaceship and within 15 seconds brought it back out, and handed it back to Jack.

"That's it, that's all you wanted to do?" said Jack.

"That's correct, and I do have the answer to your question."

Next to Aliqa a screen appeared which again showed Lava inside a laboratory.

On the screen was a deep frozen area inside the SYIRUX-82 ship, where nitrogen gas tubes were all over the place, as Lava came inside the glass doors and entered the freezer. It was a video surveillance shot of the lab.

Lava entered the cold domain and went right to the glass shelves. There, she saw a black open boxed container holding glowing green, blue, yellow and red tubes. The transparent tubes were filled with liquid and had different types of coding. She put her fingers through it as the bar code lit up and turned its cover into a picture of a monkey. She then touched other bottles as they turned into a Turtle, lizard and fish. She then put her finger on to a black tube, but the bar code didn't glow. She took out a little device from her pocket and lit it over the black bottle but still nothing happened.

She got on her microphone.

"Zelta D1 please identify the object I am holding in my hand," asked Lava.

A female voice faded on the intercom, which was inside the cold room.

"I am sorry, object unidentified please use the coding identification log on the main servers," D1 replied.

"When was the object put on sector 42NX section 82?" Lava asked.

"1.2695nx ~ dx1 light years ago," said D1.

"What about the other tubes on the rack?" asked Lava.

"1.136465dx lights years ago," D1 replied.

Lava put the tube back into the rack and pressed a button on the side of the box, but nothing happened. She pressed it several times, then picked a manual box from the top of the shelf and shoved the unidentified tube inside and walked out.

'Where are you taking that?" asked one of the scientists on the ship who was passing by the lab.

"Captain wants to see it," said Lava.

"Is it check-out time yet?" he asked.

"It's beyond that," said Lava as she closed the door and walked away.

She then came back to the same video clip depicting her carrying the black box outside.

She exited the ship and came walking outside and just like before, when KYIRUX lost its power, she trampled on the rock as her leg slipped.

Lava fell over the ground as the black box landed right next to her. Everyone came running as she quickly got up with the help of her hands. While getting up, her palm got scratched on a rock as a single strain of blood was planted on the surface.

Pascal came over and held her up.

"Are you ok?" he asked.

"Yes, I am very sorry," Lava replied.

"Don't be," he said.

Pascal picked up the black box and opened it up, while it leaked from the bottom, as several drops landed on the ground.

"Oh no…," Pascal suddenly said.

"What captain, what happened?" Lava asked as she was now emotionally scared about the situation.

"It's my fault. I didn't realize that I changed the position of the box, which was containing the Thiroglax tube. I only wanted to capture this mysterious gas for further examination."

Pascal and everyone around him closed their eyes in sorrow.

The drops of chemical merged in with the blood of Lava.

"What is wrong captain?" said Lava as she became increasingly worried.

"We have exposed our genes to this planet." he replied, as he looked straight into Lava's eyes.

She looked down in disappointment.

"But nothing has broken on the ground captain," said another astronaut.

"I already noticed the rock with your blood on it. This is why I always want everyone to wear their protective suites at all times, please take this box inside."

He took the video pen out of Robot's hands and opened its chip.

"DEX brings the computer from section 445XEESD8 for FCU situation," said Pascal who felt a bit detached from himself.

A door opened to a room where DEX, one of the astronauts, came inside. The room was glowing blue, on the corner were four levels of rack that were carrying the exact same copy of the KYIRUX computer. He went and picked the one that Pascal instructed him to bring outside.

All the pilots and robots were now going inside the ship except Lava and Pascal as DEX came flying onboard with high velocity. He handed Pascal the computer.

He took the computer in his hand and put the small video chip inside it after pressing some codes that brought out a chip holder. He programmed the computer again as it suddenly self locked and covered itself with a total black shell.

He put the computer down on the ground where it shot out steam from underneath. A green laser got turned on at the bottom of the device, while suddenly it created a deep opening below. The computer merged itself beneath the surface of the Earth.

Pascal's face could be seen from below the hole as the device went deeper and deeper into the ground.

"Goodbye friends, we shall meet you at the gates," said Pascal as the soil came over the computer.

"And this is how your planet was filled with life and beauty around it," Aliqa explained as she showed her own graphics on how everything began evolving on Earth.

From that drop of blood that was mixed with the genes created small amoebas, which several years later increased into billions and trillions of microscopic cells.

Slowly, depending upon the climate and environment of each region, the section of the land began to transform into different types of insects and microscopic germs. After hundreds of years passed, a turtle type animal began to emerge amongst these insects and then fully developed into a turtle, within those turtles they started to lose their shell, and the legs disappear and turned into snakes. Some of the other insects that traveled far to other land transformed themselves into feathery creatures as they morphed themselves into birds. It also showed how some of the birds with feather turned into just land birds like roosters, turkeys, ostriches and dinosaurs.

In the eclipse of time the two moons of Earth collided into one another, as a huge piece fell on Earth's surface. The gazing dinosaurs looked up at the falling peace of Moon that quickly wiped out everything. The boiling moon morphed itself again into a round ball of gray sand, and kept taking all the hits from asteroids and space junk.

Jack, Jay, Clark, John and Laura all had tears in their eyes, while Michael and Lisa had their eyes fixed on the alien lady as they smiled at her.

Michael put his hand out to try and touch her. Aliqa realized the little guy's request.

She gently walked over to Michael, and with her hands touched the soft and small hands of Michael. She reached into the pocket of her suit and took out a very beautiful looking locket of a planet, which was not like Earth but had similar land marks. Lisa also spread her arms out as Aliqa hugged Lisa with love and care. She too got the same pendant from her.

"Keep this with you, it will teach you all the things you want to learn about us and this Universe, Lisa and Michael," said Aliqa in a very pleasant manner.

"Come on Jack, let me show you our ship," said Aliqa as she held Jack's hand and started to walk towards the ship. Everyone followed as the alien creatures were very welcoming.

Jack held the computer in his hand as he curiously explored every inch of the alien ship. Clark and Jay were holding each other as they could not believe their eyes. This was a dream come true.

Staples Center, Los Angeles

A mysterious man in a brown suit came to the door as two military guards stood in front.

He walked inside while the sound of a huge crowd began to fade in. The closer this man got the louder the crowd screamed.

His hand cut through the curtain and saw a jam-packed crowd outside the Staples center (Los Angeles). In the front rows, celebrities, sports and political figures were sitting with drinks and popcorn in their hands.

There were hugs and kisses being exchanged amongst aliens and humans. It was like an after-party of a successful Hollywood premier, but the crowd went even more nuts as Jack Crawford walked up onto the stage.

At the very front of the crowd, Aliqa, Mrs. Laura Crawford, Michael, Lisa, Clark, Jay and John enjoyed their VIP seats. John was busy eating from a large bucket of fried Chicken.

Jack glanced at Laura and put his left hand in the air where he showed his diamond ring to her and to the world. She too waved her left hand at him and showed her own rock; which apparently was naturally bigger than Jack's.

The world was in celebration with the Universe.

Behind Jack was perhaps the biggest plasma screen ever, about 10 stories high. Similar presentations were being given in every single corner of the world. It was also being broadcast on every single television set around the globe.

Jack got up to the stand and started punching in some codes on a laptop and didn't say a word.

The lights went out in the entire city, while only the glowing reflections of the aliens' suites were visible. The crowd suddenly became quiet.

Then, one by one, each alien pressed a button on their chest as the lights on their suits dimmed and finally faded out.

Suddenly everything was dark and then, Pascal came onto the screen, looking at the entire crowd as he once did with Jack and spoke.

"My name is Pascal," the magical words froze everyone onto their seats.

While Pascal spoke to the world, the KYIRUX computer that was behind the huge secure screen started transmitting data, that no one was aware of at the time. A small screen came out that showed a pulsing dot with a diagram of our solar system. It showed a dot coming from planet Jupiter as it connected with Earth. Something awfully peculiar was afoot. Aadesh, who was standing backstage with the computer, carefully looked at it. He knew that there was only one human with the knowledge and wits to solve this new crisis.

"JACK!!!" yelled Aadesh as he ran onto the stage.

What was this animation all about? What purpose did it have at that particular time? It's up to Jack and his team to figure it out.

"THE HIDDEN HISTORY" PART II KYIRUX

(March 11th 2011)

"Man finally takes the journey to outer planets, and, is stunned!"

INSPIRATION IGNITED

Log on to www.KRSNovels.com for (AUTHORS BIO)

It's very common for authentic writers to come up with ideas for their subject from the most unorthodox situations. I, too, am a part of that sorority of strangers. My inspiration for writing the book came from just one word, which appeared in an undisclosed magazine.

It was an early evening, around 5:30 pm. I was visiting my uncle's house back in 2000 when the stock market was just about to crash. Usually, I had many conversations with him about the Universe, Life, spirituality and technology. With both of us being Scorpios, we went in depth on every subject. During that era I picked up a (now forgotten) magazine from his table and started browsing. There, I saw the "message" written clearly for me. The mysterious word was speaking to me. Within a matter of few seconds the entire story flashed in front of my eyes. Suddenly, my brain grew more cells and my unused muscles were awakened. I had an urge to write a novel with this unique word, at the same time the History Channel was on. There, the subject was presented on great mathematicians of the world.

I wasn't paying attention to the tube at that particular time; rather I was immensely drowned in my thoughts of this word. I wanted to write something, anything about this word. I didn't even pay attention, or was interested in talking to my uncle about any subject. There, while fully concentrating and putting my focus on the story, the name Pascal was mentioned on the television. It must have been the way the Universe felt when the big bang occurred. I had everything in front of me. From start to finish about my novel, the first thought that came to my head was the title. No sooner than I said that to myself, I had the entire story in my head. It was that simple, out of nowhere everything exploded in my head. I didn't say a word that day and ran to my car, and went back home.

It was no secret that I went straight to the computer and put the title: The Message of Pascal in bold letters at size 24 in MS- word. I wrote the first 24 pages right-there-&-then, but, halted myself, and the pace slowed down to a point where I didn't touch the novel for couple of years, actually more than 5 years. It was one of those short passion shocks, which you must fulfill and let be.

In 2006 I went to watch a very touching and motivating documentary titled "Tupac Resurrection," it was a biography of hip-hop artist Tupac Shakur. While in the middle of watching it, I realized I couldn't waste time, if I have a talent and a skill I should not sit and waste them, because this was the message given by Mr. Shakur in the documentary. He never wasted time, even in jail he wrote poems, lyrics to his music, including movie scripts.

I've been a big fan of his music, lyrics and poetry since high school. He wasn't just a rapper but a philosopher for million others and me. Once I came out of the theater I again ran to my car, hopped in and rushed home. Once in my room I began the process of finishing up my novel; from that moment on I kept writing and ended up finishing it in three months. "Thank you Mr. Tupac Shakur…" is what I said after I typed the last word of the first draft.

But, once I took up Kundalini meditation, which took me to different dimensions, and only then did I re-wrote the entire novel, and began putting soul into the evolution process of man. I am blessed to know what I know today.

12263591R00150

Made in the USA
Lexington, KY
01 December 2011